My Brother's Keeper

PW Long

Blue Ocean Press

Japan & USA

Published by:
Blue Ocean Press

Japan Office
6F & 7F TOC Daiichi Bldg.
1-8-3 Shibuya
Shibuya-ku, Tokyo, Japan 150-0002

USA Office
P.O. Box 510818
Punta Gorda, FL 33951 USA

URL: http://www.blueoceanpublications.com
Email: director@aoishima-research.org

ISBN: 978-4-902837-62-9

Table of Contents

If We Must Die
By Claude McKay

If we must die, let it not be like hogs
Hunted and penned in an inglorious spot,
While round us bark the mad and hungry dogs,
Making their mock at our accursed lot.
If we must die, O let us nobly die,
So that our precious blood may not be shed
In vain; then even the monsters we defy
Shall be constrained to honor us though dead!
O kinsmen! we must meet the common foe!
Though far outnumbered let us show us brave,
And for their thousand blows deal one death-blow!
What though before us lies the open grave?
Like men we'll face the murderous, cowardly pack,
Pressed to the wall, dying, but fighting back!

Prologue

Palm Haven Village

The avenue into the village, appropriately named "Royal Palm Avenue," is bordered by royal palms on each side. Two pools with spraying fountains greet those who approach the residences. Ibis with bright white feathers forage around the pond in a group, looking like a flock of busy birds enjoying a picnic; mocking birds are heard in different morning birdsong throughout the swaying palm fronds. A clear blue sky overlooks the perfectly landscaped grounds. Palm Haven Village is said to be a paradise for retired seniors with elegant accommodations and all of the intellectual, fitness, and recreational amenities for which one could wish. Some joke that living at the Village is like being on a first-class ocean liner, a cruise through every day of one's life at the Village.

A trio emerges from a very long limousine in front of their new residence, "Serenity View," breathing in the warm Florida air and releasing sighs and words of great satisfaction.

"Bro, this is real Florida."

"I agree wholeheartedly -- not like living in the country in Cottondale and Greenwood."

"I think I can feel the breeze off of the Gulf already." They all laugh and give each other high fives.

Word had already reached the Palm Haven community that three single African American men would be taking up residency; two were widowered and one never married. Most gossip is about the gentleman taking care of the financial responsibilities for the group, a successful farmer in North Florida. Or, he is a multi-millionaire who made his fortune in Detroit before retiring to Florida.

The three exquisitely dressed African American gentlemen are graciously greeted by the staff as they move into their new home. Daniel Austin Baker (DB), tall, light complexioned with light brown eyes and wavy, gray-streaked hair has the appearance and manner of a college professor. His brother, the Reverend Edward Baker, has the same complexion and features but is a bit rotund. he wears a hearing aid and walks with the aid of a cane. Raymond Edwards (Rabbit as he is nicknamed) is tall, with a copper-colored complexion and his straight silver hair pulled back into a ponytail. Rabbit appears to be the youngest and the most fit of the trio.

DB has built an empire now enjoyed and managed by his great-grand nieces and nephews. It was at the urging of DB's grandniece, Annabelle, after his heart attack a year ago, that he give up the worry of the farms and his businesses in Marianna to the younger set and finally enjoy the type of life he deserves. DB is recognized and honored as the source for the Baker family's social status and wealth. Annabelle insisted that at 95 years of age he should spend his last years in as much peace and comfort as he can tolerate. Annabelle researched and found Palm Haven Village on Florida's Gulf coast. Here, with the luxury and the amenities, Uncle Daniel, Grandpa Edward, and Cousin Rabbit will have no worries, only a life they deserve because of hard work and dedication to family and others.

Once the trio is moved into their luxurious accommodations -- DB a two-bedroom apartment and Edward and Rabbit into their one-bedroom apartments -- they take time to observe and think about this new life. DB stands on his lanai, looks out upon the smoothly flowing pond and thinks to himself that now in his last years he doesn't have a care in the world, only peace. He takes a deep breath, feels invigorated, truly alive and ready for this new adventure at ninety-five years old.

The trio is welcomed and settles into the village. Each has his own area of interest; DB enjoys the book groups, Philo Club and lectures. Edward becomes very involved in the religious services, takes up gardening and woodworking, while folks are shocked by the athletic prowess of Rabbit, who swims daily, plays tennis, golf and enjoys a game of poker with the men. After five years, the trio are the most popular members of the Village, and a special surprise awaits Daniel or DB as he is called by family and friends.

Book I

Memories

100 Years Old

Gold, silver, and platinum balloons float above the table on which sits a large sheet cake with blue and white cream frosting. Three sparkling candles, 1,0,0 graced the center of the cake, underneath is spelled in frosting, **Happy Birthday Daniel.** Two dozen gray-haired elders, standing alone, others on walkers, and some leaning against the mahogany armoire filled with priceless china and figurines surround the table, cheer and whistle as the guest of honor is escorted into the room. Immediately the 84-year-old pianist, Josie, dressed in a lavender satin, begins to play "Happy Birthday", on the Baby Grand piano, and the group bursts into song as they serenade the centenarian, his face covered by a broad smile.

"Happy Birthday to you! Happy Birthday to you!

"Happy Birthday Dear Daniel!

"We wish you a 100 more!"

The crowd breaks into uproarious laughter as DB is now prodded to make a wish and blow out the three candles. He closes his eyes momentarily, leans back, takes a big breath, leans forward and blows out all three of the candles. The crowd roars in approval. After blowing out the candles, DB is escorted to the seat of honor, where he is presented with a tee shirt which reads, "The World's Most

Handsome 100-Year-Old", a coffee mug with "100 years old" in gold letters, and a gold crown is placed upon his head by Josie. She gives him a peck on the cheek. He gives her a flirtatious wink and sexily whispers "Thank you!" Josie blushes.

At 100, is still a very handsome man. Tall, slender, a thick head of white hair, a thin face, finely chiseled features, lined with a white beard. His light brown complexion shows few winkles, and a blue circle outlines his light brown eyes. DB is sportily dressed as usual, navy slacks, a blue and white striped shirt, a white linen jacket, and brown leather loafers.

"Speech, speech," the crowd chants. They move to the gold sofas and armchairs placed around the room. DB clears his throat and says, "Thank you all so very much for celebrating my 100 years of this earth with me. Thank you to the staff who has prepared this wonderful celebration for me. I am truly a grateful man. God has granted me, can you imagine, 100 years, with few health issues but I have survived. "The crowd laughs. "He gave me a loving wife and a devoted brother and friend, wonderful great-grandnieces and nephews. I have had a good life. That life has made it possible for me to live my last years in this wonderful retirement home. I love it here, I love all of you. Most of what I desired in life has been granted to me. Again, thank you." Tears fill his eyes. His brother Edward and Rabbit pat him on the back. They begin to weep as well. The three men hold each other in a tight embrace.

"Surprise, surprise," says Pam, the perky red-headed receptionist. She covers his eyes. "Now open." A video plays, "Happy Birthday to Grand-uncle and Great-grand-uncle Danial." The entire extended family in on the video wishing DB birthday wishes, from the oldest to the youngest. As a parting wish, they ask DB to record his memories of those 100 years. He agrees to their request. Tears gush from DB's eyes, as he trembles with joy.

A buffet table is laden with appetizers of all sorts. The celebration goes on into the night.

As the trio leaves the party, they gush with joy, wide grins and eyes sparkle and gleam, their movements and giggles are reminiscent of young boys. When the elevator door shuts. They squeal with excitement. " Man that was some birthday party." "They acted and treated you like a king."

"Well, hell, man he is a king", the trio bellows at the joke. Both Edward and Rabbit hug DB, " man you are the best."

The trio decides to have a nightcap to celebrate and retires for the night in DB's apartment, where when they are too tired to stay up any longer will enjoy the twin beds in his guest room.

"Bro, tonight's the perfect time to start with those memories," suggests Edward.

"I agree", says Rabbit, pouring each a drink and getting comfortable to talk about all the years. "I really want this very fortunate generation to hear about all that we went through in Detroit to bring them where they are now. We had a good life, but there were troublesome times." They give each other high fives.

"I guess while we are all in a celebratory mood, that we remember as best we old men can," says DB "Where do I start?"

"Start from us having to leave those crackers in Greenwood before we had trouble. The old man got us out of there just in time, bless him," says Edward with a frown.

"Okay, down memory lane we will go," agrees Daniel and for the night and into the early morning hours the trio listened, laughed and told their sides of the story from Greenwood to Detroit and back to Greenwood.

1915
The Magnificent Orange Sky

Ten-year-old DB stands still, entranced by the night sky in the distance. The darkness and even the stars have disappeared, dwarfed by a massive bowl of bright orange. He flinches and steps back slightly when yellow streaks shoot through the orange bowl. He has never seen such a magnificent sight before. With wide eyes, mouth gaping, barely taking a breath, he does not hear his mother calling him. Twice she calls, but he is fully taken with the orange bowl. Finally, his mother taps him on the shoulder, but he remains polarized by the sight. He is startled a few minutes later by his father's harsh rebuke. "Boy, didn't you hear your mama calling you? Why didn't you move when she came out here? Get in the house now."

DB takes one last peek as his father pushes him through the front door and sharply closes it behind him.

DB's siblings, eight-year-old Edward, and the six-year-old twins, Sally and Susie, watch in silence. "All of you get in the bed now, don't worry about a bath or putting on night clothes, sleep in what you are wearing, just blow out the candle and go to sleep, and I mean right now." Rev. Daniel Baker is still in his no-nonsense voice. The children give each other questioning glances but follow their father's orders. They are confused, not understanding Papa's tone or urgency. Papa is strict but never this harsh. The boys climb into their bed and the girls into theirs. Rev. Baker closes the door.

As soon as the door is closed, DB and Edward slip out of bed and go to the door to listen. Their parents are talking softly so they can't hear much, but they do recognize that Rev. Baker has taken the shotgun from its rack. Hearing his footsteps, they quickly scamper back to bed.

The next morning, their mother Lillian rouses the children early. "Time to get ready for church." What she said next is strange, unexpected, and totally out of character for their mother. "The washbowl is ready, just wash your face, brush your teeth, and change into church clothes and shoes."

"Where is papa?" the girls ask.

"Deacon Jones picked him up a while ago."

DB's curiosity is getting the best of him now, and being the oldest, he feels he has the right to know what is going on so that the younger children won't be afraid.

"Mama, is something wrong?" He asks somewhat shyly, not wanting to overstep his bounds.

"No, dear, everything is fine for now. No more questions, we need to go. The Sneed's will be here in a few minutes to pick us up. "

"But, Mama, why are you and papa acting this way?" Wide-eyed and concerned, he feels anxiety about the "for now." Does it mean that there is something outside that is wrong? He can barely contain himself.

"DB, you will learn everything you need to know in service this morning. Now let's get out on the porch to wait. "The Sneed's arrive, the wagon loaded with husband, wife, and six children. Mrs. Baker climbs in the front with Mr. and Mrs. Sneed, and the Baker children squeeze in with their friends, looking at each other with questions in their eyes but not talking. They've never ridden in silence the three miles to the Zion A.M.E. church in Greenwood, Florida, a small rural village near Marianna.

As they enter the little wooden church filled with wooden benches and a simple pulpit, DB notices that the congregation is unusually quiet. Seems as though folks are praying rather than greeting and talking to each other about their week as usual. To DB, the silence and the strange behavior of the adults feels like a weight in his stomach. At 11:10, Rev. Baker exits the small room at the back of the church with four of his deacons. DB notices that Deacon Jones gives his father a brown cloth bag that his father places near the Bible. The bag appears heavy, and DB is mightily curious.

The small choir of six women and four men take their seats. Miss Polly, a gray-haired woman of at least 80 and a Mother of the Church begins to line a hymn. After each verse, the choir sings and the congregation follow with "Nobody knows the trouble I've seen, no…body but Jesus." Women in the pews begin to weep openly and call "Jesus, Jesus."

When the hymn is finished, Rev. Baker asks the congregation to remain standing. From the back of the church come James Green, in clothes dirty and tattered, followed by his wife Ethel and three small children. Each has the appearance of trees walking, no feelings, just hollow souls. Everyone moves over to make room for the family. Ethel Green begins to wail, her cries echoing in the hearts and minds of the silent church. Children begin to cry. Mr. Green holds his head in his hands.

And DB is still confused; why are the Greens in church dressed so shabbily?

In a few seconds, his answer comes. He hears his father's deep prayer voice. "Dear Father God, we sinners come before you asking for your mercy and your grace. Last night, Satan, dressed in the sheets of the Klu Klux Klan, burned the home and fields of our brother and his family. You, my good Father, saved their lives by covering them with your mighty protection in the woods. Merciful Father, they may be bruised, battered and without a home, but they will survive, you have kept them in Your mercy. Father God, I ask You to direct me to the Bible lesson that will give meaning and hope to us this morning. This I ask in the name and in mercy of our Lord and Savior Jesus Christ. Amen."

The congregation sits as the Rev. Baker closes his eyes, holds his head upward, and stretches out his hands asking God for direction. He opens his Bible, places his finger on a scripture and begins to read. "From Psalm 44, Verse 5-8: Through You, we will push back our adversaries. Through Your name we will trample down those who rise up against us. For I will not trust in my bow, nor will my sword save me. But You have saved us from our adversaries. And You have put to shame those who hate us. In God we have boasted all day long. And we will give thanks to Your name all day long. Selah."

Amens sing out over the entire congregation. Men and women stand waving hands. Some woman overcome with emotion faint. But DB sits in silence, feeling the shame again. His cheeks begin to burn as tears flow. At once, his body begins shaking. Mother Jones comes over and wraps him in her arms. "Tell Jesus, tell Jesus, let Jesus take your burden." DB gently pushes her arms aside and runs out of the church. He stops and rests under the oak tree in the cemetery where his grandfather, the Rev. Isaac Baker is buried. He bends himself into his face and chest, his body now shaking uncontrollably, and he asks over and over, "How could I see the beauty in such an ugly act?"

He realizes that the orange bowl which bewitched him was the fire rising from Mr. Green's house and farm. "What have I done? Can God ever forgive me for seeing beauty in such a sinful act? I pretended not to hear Mama or Papa, just so I could watch the orange bowl."

By now, DB's mother has come out to look for him. She reaches for him and holds him tightly in her arms.

"Honey, what is it? I know you are scared and upset, but Jesus will work this out. Farmer Green and his family have a place to stay. Your papa and the deacons will take up enough money for them to get back on their feet. Our whole church will help them."

DB. continues to stare into space, seeing something his mother cannot fathom.

"Darling, please don't be afraid. Our family will be fine. Papa and the deacons are going to work out a plan to protect all of us. Do you trust Papa?"

"Yes, mam," DB says softly.

"Then please be strong, you are the big brother, be brave for the little ones. They believe in you. You must always be strong for the younger ones, for your family. You are a Baker, the son of Daniel Baker, Sr., and your grandfather, Rev. Isaac Baker. These men knew what to do for our family and the community. Through their faith they used their power to protect those who felt they had no power. Did you know that your grandfather, Rev. Isaac was a free man who came down South to fight with the Union army? "

"No, mam, Papa never told us the story." DB looks as though what he is hearing is incredulous.

His sense of shame mellows as he considers his role as a Baker man to attain power despite being colored. He does not understand yet, nor will he for some time, how this need for power will become the focus of his life.

After service, the women lay out the usual Sunday after service fare -- fried chicken, beef stew, potato salad, macaroni and cheese, sweet potato pie, coconut cake, and lemonade. The men, women, and children all eat at their respective tables; for men, women, and the children's tables. The women talk softly among themselves, the men in serious voices of how to help the Greens. The children gobble their food and rush off to play among the graves in the cemetery. DB sits alone boxed in by the residue of his guilt and shame. He berates himself for making fun of the Green's clothing this morning but mostly keeps asking himself how he ever saw beauty in the evil act.

After the school principal, his family and a few others leave, Rev. Baker, Deacon Jones, and a small group of men soon depart to the small room in back of the church.

DB yearns to know what they are discussing, but he has to ride home in the wagon.

Rev. Baker does not return home until the next morning. DB awakens as he hears the front door leaps out of bed to greet him.

"Papa, where have you been? I worried about you."

"Son, don't worry about me, Jesus has my back. Deacon Jones and I had some business to take care of with the others. Things are going to work out fine. You get back into bed and get some sleep."

DB's mother is now up and guides him back to bed. As soon as he feels it safe, and that all of his siblings are still asleep, he tiptoes back to the door to eavesdrop.

"How did it go, honey?' asks Mrs. Baker. "I'm making you some coffee and grits, eggs, sausage and biscuits for breakfast."

"Thank you." He hugs her for a long time and finally lets his wife go and sits down with a sigh. "Everything went well. We have a plan in place. It will take about a week, then Moses will lead his people to safety."

"I love you, Rev. Moses Baker." They both laugh and at first DB is relieved – everything is okay. But he hears something in the laugh he suddenly realizes he's never heard before and is not sure what to make of the unsteadiness of it. He is unable to hear anymore as Mama is noisy making breakfast, and like their son, the two of them are silent in their own thoughts.

Let My People Go

The burning out of the Green family and another prosperous colored farmer make Daniel Sr. worry about his family's safety and their future in Greenwood. The Rev. Daniel Baker Sr. is one of the successful colored farmers in Jackson County, Florida. The son of an enslaved mother and slave-holding father, he was given 100 acres of farmland when they were freed. His father, the Judge Felix Russell was a highly respected member of the white elite who held enough power to protect his colored son. With his father now deceased, and whites attacking and taking colored homesteads, Daniel Sr. is increasingly preoccupied.

Rev. Daniel Baker hears from his cousin in Detroit that the pastor of a small AME church there is retiring and that with Rev. Baker's current position and status in his AME church in FL, he would be a perfect candidate for the position. The congregation, looking for a young enthusiastic leader to take his place, will have to look no longer if Rev. Baker takes over. And, the cousin says, many of the colored leaving Florida would join the church.

The beginning of World War I in 1914 shut off of European immigration to America, and a labor shortage in the North provided opportunities for colored workers. The Chicago Defender, a colored paper, is continuously printing stories about colored being recruited and finding good pay up North. Word gets around that Green has in his possession the newspaper and is encouraging colored sharecroppers to go North; as a result, he is punished by the KKK. Colored make up the labor force in the area, and white landowners do not stand for any loss of cheap cotton pickers. They begin efforts to intimidate and restrict travel of the colored.

Rev. Baker knows that he has to devise a plan to leave the area, and somehow not lose his property to whites once he is gone.

On Friday, porters on the local train from Jacksonville drop off the Florida Sentinel, the colored newspaper. The front page is alarming. Presiding Elder Watson, a leading member of the Republican Party in Florida during Reconstruction, has been killed in an accident, funeral services to be held the following Saturday in Jacksonville. The news spreads fast, and every colored person in Marianna, Greenwood, and Cottondale is made aware of it.

Rev. Baker and Deacon Jones visit every A.M.E. church in the area, reminding them of the important role of Elder Watson in assisting colored people during those promising, then dark, times. During Reconstruction in Florida, the colored Methodists were the leaders of the Republican Party. Watson along with other pastors becomes well-known in political circles. If one wants to get into politics in Florida, becoming a colored Methodist is the ticket.

On Sunday morning, Rev. Baker, Deacon Jones, and a few other of the deacons emerge from the small room in the back of the church before service with triumphant faces. DB watches carefully, his mind spinning, wondering what the men talk about every time they go in there.

And then Rev. Baker begins the service differently than DB was used to, asking Deacon Jones' wife Hattie to lead the congregation in a special song.

DB frowns as he watches.

She begins." Go down Moses, way down in Egypt land, tell all the Pharaohs to let my people go," Church members leap to their feet, clap and sway to the music. They chant over and over "Let my people go." Eyes tearful the week before are bright and sparkly this morning. Members begin the "holy dance," bouncing from foot to foot, as they sing the hymn again and again. Some so filled with the Spirit faint, and women dressed in white fan them and place smelling salts under their nostrils. For almost a half-hour the exhilaration continues, all the children now dancing around the benches. Finally, Rev. Baker waves his arms for the congregation to sit.

Again, not in the usual manner in which things are done, Rev. Baker gives no sermon but talks about the virtues of Elder Watson. Then, in his most serious tone and pounding on the pulpit, Rev. Baker demands that every family or at least a member of every family attend the funeral on Saturday. "Don't let money be a reason for not honoring this great man, the church will provide. We will have to leave on the Friday evening for Jacksonville and return on Sunday. Let your boss man know that you will need one day off to serve the Lord. You must come dressed for the funeral, wear your mourning clothes, but bring another set of clothes to wear back home. And very important, bring food to share for Friday night and to share with everyone after the funeral on Saturday. Sisters, you fry up as many chickens as you can; make some greens, beans, and cornbread. Yes, bake some pound cakes and pies. Make jars of lemonade. We will feed the masses in Jacksonville."

The congregation roars with excited approval, then turns to each other in eager conversation. "Now," interrupts the minister, "let us all come to the altar in prayer to ask our merciful God to bless us as we plan and depart for the funeral of our leader on next Saturday."

The congregation moves toward the altar, joins in prayer, and receives a short sermon before dismissal.

DB smiles to himself. Going to the funeral and all will be a great trip, both for the family and the church, but something still puzzles him. Why do Papa and the deacons have so much church business since last Sunday visiting all the people from the church? Can't be that many sick and shut-in to have to visit. What is going on?

That very Sunday night, once home, some of DB's questions are answered. Papa calls a family prayer circle as he often does, asking especially for God's protection and safety as they progress through the week. Then more comes, but still not enough for it seems to befuddle DB even more.

He and Edward are to help Papa pick cotton all week and put it in bales so he can take it to market in Marianna on Friday morning. The twins are to help DB and Edward pick all the ripe fruit from the trees as well as help Mama fold clothes. Mama is cooking day and night. Aunt Sadie and Uncle Joe come to help mother kill all the chickens and take them to their house. What DB does not realize is that most of the congregation is engaged in the same activity.

On Friday morning, after returning from Marianna to sell his cotton, Rev. Baker gathers the children, blesses them all with Holy Oil and asks for God's protection as they take the trip to Jacksonville. By now, ninety percent of the Zion A.M.E. congregation, dressed in mourning clothes and carrying bags of clothing and food, is making its way past Marianna. Men beg off work, and if refused permission, lose the day's pay, saying it is their Christian duty to attend the funeral of their leader.

Whites snicker and talk among themselves about the strange ways of those crazy niggas.

By evening, the procession of wagons reaches Jacksonville and the train depot. Horses and wagons are suddenly being given away for almost nothing to men and families not taking the trip. DB is bewildered, but the men are too busy to pay any attention to him, so he gets no answers. When he enters the colored waiting room with his family, a flurry of people laughing, talking, faces sparkling with joy confound him even more.

He finally gets into his father's way and asks, "Papa, are we going to spend the night here in this crowded waiting room? Where will we get ready for the funeral?"

"Son, we are ready for funeral Remember last Sunday's sermon about Moses leading the Jews out of Egypt? "answers his father.

"Yes, but what does…?" DB suddenly looks closely at his papa. "We are not going to Rev. Watson's funeral, are we?"

"DB, we are going to our freedom land. We are taking the first train out of here early in the morning to Atlanta and then on to Detroit."

A huge smile covers DB's face as he hugs his father with all his might. He breaks into laughter. His eyes and his smile signal such pride and delight in his papa, and then as he looks around, to all the men in the waiting room with their families. He watches the Green family, dressed in new mourning clothes, laughing and talking with the others. He knows with some newly discovered instinct that it is only his father who could think up such a scheme.

That night in bed, DB begins to see his papa more clearly in his mind. He is not just a father; he is a very smart man, able to figure out things other than family, crop and church. He is saving their people from violence, and fire, and probably death.

Though DB, being who he is, worries what will happen to those who stay behind. He worries, too, about being forced off the train somewhere.

The following Friday, the Florida Sentinel prints a front-page apology to their readers. The editor apologizes for providing readers with incorrect information, and the trouble caused to families coming to Jacksonville for the funeral. "The Presiding Elder was injured but did not die in the accident. Jesus answers prayers."

There was no mention of a caravan of colored who left Jacksonville heading to Detroit on the train the prior Saturday.

Miss Josephine

Edward picks up a photo of Miss Josephine and DB." Look at that smile, Miss Josephine really loved you like a son."

"I say so too," adds Rabbit.

"Yes, she was like a second mother to me. Reminded much of Granny Ruby Pearl, they were so much alike.

"Man, she turned you out, got you into the numbers racket when you were a mere baby." They all laugh.

"Well, I wasn't exactly a baby, I was already sixteen."

"What gets me is that Pop never said a word. In those days, old people, elders as they called them, had the last word. But I wonder if he ever suspected?"

"Hell, everybody in his church was playing the numbers except him. Even old Deacon McCray stopped in the barbershop every Saturday to play. He played big time, a dollar every week."

"You are joking, old religious Lord Jesus is watching, Deacon McCray?"

"Yep, every week." DB chuckles and looks up as if trying to recall a memory.

"Did I ever tell you guys' about how Miss Josephine started me in the numbers racket?

The two look at each other and smile. Edward says,

"Yes, man, but we love to hear it. I know one thing, she was one damn good teacher, made us all rich and you especially. A millionaire."

DB proceeds to tell the story.

****

Rev. Baker has just finished saying grace when there is a knock on the door. Lillian Baker jumps up to answer it. To her surprise, it is Miss Josephine.

"Well, hello Miss Josephine, you are just in time for dinner," she says as she shows the elderly woman in.

"Oh, no, I am so sorry to interrupt your meal. I will come back."

"No mam, you are not disturbing us one bit, let me pour you a glass of tea?"

"Nothing, my dear, I just wanted to speak to you for a moment about DB."

At that DB's heart feels like it will jump out of his chest; his mouth fills with saliva, his eyes are as wide as saucers. He sits as a chair.

By now, the women have made their way to the kitchen.

"Rev. Baker and Lillian, you know I am getting more and more feeble. I am already 80 years old and I am beginning to feel it. Can't do things around the house like I used to. Charles took care of everything I needed a male to do when he was alive. Bless his soul."

Rev. and Mrs. Baker, smile understandingly.

"I just came to ask a favor, if you will."

"Yes, mam," said Rev. Baker.

"Well, I see DB is growing so nice and tall and he is a smart young man. Always very manner able. I was just wondering if he could help me out with things at my house." She says this more as a declaration than a question. Both Bakers nod.

"If he can come over each morning before he goes to school and come to my house on his lunch break, he can really help me out. I will make him a sandwich and you know I always keep a pot of soup on the stove when it is chilly. And of course, I bake the best pound cake and sugar cookies in the neighborhood, all of the children like them."

Rev. Baker immediately replies, "Yes, mam, he will do that for you, won't you DB?"

Shocked by everything that is happening, DB's mouth gapes open without a sound coming out.

"Did you hear me, DB?" asks his father.

"Yes, sir, I mean yes, mam, I will gladly help you out, Miss Josephine."

"That's mighty fine of you, young man. I will give you a quarter a week for helping me."

Lillian quickly replies, "Oh no, Miss Josephine, we do for our elders, and we don't charge them, that is what we are supposed to do." Miss Josephine smiles.

"Well, young man, I will see you in the morning before you go to school." Speaking to Rev. and Lillian. promise he will never be late returning to his studies. I'll just get him to do one or two little things in the morning and finish up at lunchtime. Thank you so much. You have raised a fine son."

Lillian walks Miss Josephine to the door. Rev. Baker smiles at DB. "See what happens when you are respectful of your elders? They really notice, and you are doing God's will."

DB still speechless from the encounter can only nod his head in agreement. He eats his in silence, tasting nothing.

"Don't you want another helping of these green beans and potatoes? They are mighty good," says Rev. Baker.

"No thank you, sir, I better get to bed a little earlier."

"Yes, you are going to have to start going to bed a little earlier young man, so that you can spend at least a half-hour with Miss Josephine before you go to school," agrees his mother.

DB nods his head yes, relieved that he is not in trouble but thoughts are racing through his mind like a runaway locomotive. *What is going on? Why did Miss Josephine come over here?*

There is something however, that DB finds intriguing about Miss Josephine. She reminds him of his mother's mother and his grandmother Ruby Pearl named for a rebellious enslaved woman that started a revolt on a plantation in South Carolina. DB would sit for hours and listen to stories about the rebellious Ruby. Now he readies himself to sit at the feet of Miss Josephine.

DB barely gets to sleep before it is time to get ready for his new crazy day.

Number Are Dream Makers

Miss Josephine opens the door just as DB is getting ready to knock. Her round face is covered with one of the biggest and brightest smiles he has ever seen.

"I wanted to tell you so badly last night but I couldn't."

Confused, he asks, "What is it Miss Josephine?" She grabs him and hugs him so tightly that he can barely breathe.

"Your number hit yesterday," she squeals.

"What?" DB can barely believe his ears.

"You, young man, just won yourself $6"

DB stands with his mouth open half unbelieving, but the $6 is a fortune, so he recovers quickly. "So, I better play a dollar today," he says grinning.

Miss Josephine brooks no silliness. "No sir, you are not going to play any m11ore numbers. You had your chance and you won. Now, Miss Josephine is going to let you learn the fine art of the numbers racket."

DB's tongue flies out of his mouth and he gazes at Miss Josephine in disbelief. Isn't he too young for this?

"I thought you agreed to help this old lady with her work."

"I did, Miss Josephine, but I thought I would be mopping and dusting for you."

"Nonsense, I can do that myself. What I need is somebody to make sure my counting and slips are correct. I have been miscounting a little bit lately, and I don't want to lose this good job I have as a number's writer."

DB stands perfectly still, almost frozen in place.

"Come on in to the kitchen, let me show you where the business takes place."

DB follows her, first noticing the white print curtains with a rooster on them, the rooster cookie jar, red, brown, and yellow roosters in the dish safe. But then he cannot believe his eyes, all he can do is stare. Moving closer to the table he is dazzled by stacks of pennies, nickels, dimes, quarters, and a few dollars. He stares at the money, then at Miss Josephine, and then the money again. He has never seen this much money in one place in his life, even in the church collection basket.

"Close your mouth child and sit down. I'll get you a cup of tea. We don't have long before you have to leave for school, so I am just going to tell you a little bit about the numbers racket."

She pours DB a cup as he sits silently, staring at the fortune on the table.

"Colored folks started the numbers way back when. Things has always been tough for us. First slavery, then we was treated like slaves when we supposed to be free. Me and Mr. Charles came to Detroit from Mississippi because we heard Charles could get a good paying job in Detroit. Charles was able to get a job at the foundry. It paid the most he had ever made but it was hard and dangerous work. We done real good, was able to buy this house. Charles would not let me work outside, said it was enough for me to keep this house and keep his clothes clean. We only had one child, a little girl, but she died as a baby before we left Mississippi. It was cold in that old shack, wind came in all sides and give that poor little thing pneumonia, killed our precious baby. Never had any more, was just me and Charles. He worked five years before he got burned really bad in the foundry and died two days later. I was all alone and had to make a living. Well, knowing Charles didn't want me in white folk's homes, I looked for the next best work for me to do. A colored woman couldn't get nothing, and still can't get nothing but domestic work. A friend of mine from church whispered in my ear about a way I could stay at home and make a very good living -- writing numbers." She pats his hand. "She introduced me to the right people and that's what I been doing for the last ten years."

"Wow, you must like it," says a smiling DB.

"You got to understand one thing about the numbers. It's made for poor colored folks like us. Yes, sometimes, we lose our pennies and nickels, but if we hit we get ahead. I know folks who save enough to buy car or put a down payment on a house. It's numbers money that sends these smart kids to college. You see, for colored people, numbers is a dream maker. We can't make it in the white man's world, he won't let us in, and if we do too good, they do us like they did us in Mississippi. Burn you out and run you out of town. We caught be twixt and between, we don't know which way to go. But white folks call our numbers "nigger pennies" and think we are just wasting money. They have no idea how many coloreds got rich on running a numbers bank."

"A numbers bank?"

"I like your questions, DB. You are a smart boy. Well, the numbers banker is the man or woman who puts up all the money and has to pay off when a number hit. Now, they make their money when numbers don't hit, and they have to pay their writers, like me, and runners who bring the money and slips to them. I am a numbers writer, those children you see coming here are bringing me the numbers their folks want played." Miss Josephine picks up a numbers book. "See, I writes their name or address, the number they want played, and how much they are putting on the number here. I gives them the top and I keeps one and gives pick-up man or runner a copy. The first thing you are going to learn is how to write the numbers."

"Really, you are going to teach me how to write numbers?"

"Yes, I am young man, but I want you to remember this lesson. It ain't all about the money, although some folks get mighty rich, it's about helping poor colored folks have a chance at life, a chance to buy a car, a house, or start a business. Almost every business you see around here was started with numbers money."

"Not my daddy's store. "

"You are right son. Your daddy was a lucky colored man. He had some money when he came here and he is a preacher. Colored preachers always find a way to make money. But men like my poor Charles have to make it the best way they can. If a colored man works in the numbers racket he can have a good life if he is careful."

"Why do you have to be careful?"

"Like I told you, white folks don't want colored folks to get ahead. If they can stop the numbers racket, colored be under them again. Long as we got the numbers, we colored folks can make it." Miss Josephine stands up abruptly and walks out of the kitchen say, "Well, it looks like you better be going to school, see you at lunch time. When you come back, will be more work and less talk, you will learn as we go along. Don't forget this is our secret."

She ushered him out and close the door.

A Crucial Lesson

Slowly and meticulously, Miss Josephine teaches DB every aspect of the numbers business, from the ground up. DB is taught what to expect from Miss Josephine's regular customers, when to arrive for a pick-up, where to pick up books, and to which driver to deliver his books. Most importantly, DB must always give a copy of the transaction to his customer and keep a copy for himself, as he will get a percentage of each winning transaction.

DB makes himself comfortable on the blue velveteen sofa decorated with white crocheted covers made by Miss Josephine and prepares himself for today's lesson. As usual, Miss Josephine makes a pitcher of freshly squeezed lemonade and places in front of him a warm batch of cookies. "Don't be shy" she encourages. "Dig in, I made these butterscotch, your favorite, just for you." DB grabs a couple, takes a sip of the lemonade even better than his mother's, let's out a sigh.

When Miss Josephine opens her Bible, DB is a little taken aback. In all their times together, she has never once mentioned "The Word," as his father refers to the Bible. He shakes off uneasiness and leans back.

"Are you familiar with the story of Cain and Abel in Genesis?"

"Yeah, I know that one. But I'm not as good a Bible student as Papa was or even as Edward is," DB answers.

Miss Josephine's face is now a wry smile. "Don't worry, you don't have to memorize Bible verses." She opens her Bible, apparently exactly to the page she wants. "But let me tell you a story from Genesis 4: 1-13."

DB feels his heart pounds as his mind fills with questions and confusion as Miss Josephine begins her story.

"Cain and Abel were brothers. Cain was so jealous of his brother Abel that he killed him. Afterwards, when God asked, 'Where is Abel?' Cain said he didn't know. That's when Cain asked, 'Am I my brother's keeper?' What Cain was really asking was if he was responsible for his brother." DB listens intently.

"The answer is yes," Miss Josephine says emphatically. "Being your brother's keeper is not just protecting and providing for Edward, Billy, your mother and sisters, but other human beings who need your help."

DB nods his head in agreement but is still confused as to where this conversation is taking him in the numbers game.

Finally, the answer comes.

"Your well-being as a numbers king, which you will become because of your smarts and your heart, is bound to the well-being of those who buy your numbers, and also those in Black Bottom who will need your help whether they play or not." Miss Josephine gives DB a steady look, then thumbs her Bible to Galatians 6:2 and asks DB to read the verse.

With a tiny hesitation, he reads.

Miss Josephine responds. "While I am not a regular church goer or Bible reader, there are some lessons from the Bible to which I adhere. Now read this one." Miss Josephine turns to Matthew 25:35 and point to the line she wants.

"This is my favorite and most meaningful verse. It speaks to me as a colored woman who has the capacity through my numbers business to help others. Read this one and let me know what it means to you."

Again, DB reads. "For I was hungry, and ye gave me meat. I was thirsty, and ye gave me drink. I was a stranger, and you took me in." Eyes down to hide his bafflement, DB is eager to learn how the Bible has anything to do with gambling. Miss Josephine pours each another glass of lemonade, passes the cookie plate to DB, and begins the most crucial lesson that he will learn as he prepares to enter the numbers racket and life itself.

"The numbers racket is thought by white folks – even some colored; well, and the police but not the Tally and Jewish gangsters -- to be illegal. But for us coloreds, it is one of the only ways we can get ahead in this white man's world. The numbers provide an opportunity for a colored man by buying a dollar ticket to make sixty dollars to feed his family or pay his rent. There is a risk of course, because we have so little, a dollar's a dollar; but the numbers can help a colored man to get ahead. Don't get me wrong, no colored man should be foolish enough to spend all his paycheck trying to get rich by playing the numbers." DB listens intently. His heart is slowing its beat and he is settling into a more comfortable place in his mind.

"The numbers do something else," Miss Josephine continues. "They provide jobs for colored men and women. Those folks from across the water don't want to see us colored get a job, they make it hard for us, say too many of us are flooding Detroit, taking 'their jobs'. So, we have to look out for ourselves."

Miss Josephine looks DB squarely in the eye. "So DB, why do you think Miss Josephine is telling you this?" DB takes a breath and hopes some answer will spill from his lips. He has already surmised that it must have something to do with looking out for your brother or other colored folks. "I have a duty to take care of my colored folks," he replies.

Miss Josephine smiles briefly. "As a numbers man, especially if you are a bank, you can become very wealthy, even a millionaire like those folks in Chicago and Harlem. You can have a great life, live just like white folks in a big house, have a nice car, wear fancy clothes, eat all the good food you've ever dreamed of, and take luxurious vacations." She takes a sip, wipes her lips, and proceeds. "But there is another side. A good numbers man not only looks out for his individual people, he gives to community organizations, he helps the poor, he provides housing for homeless people escaping from the south, he even pays for folks' funerals when the family can't afford to. He can do all of this because he puts his money in legal businesses -- buys a store, a barbershop, sells land, builds apartments, he cleans up what the white folks call 'dirty' money by providing for his people."

She peers at DB over her glass. "Any questions? No? Okay." And keeps talking. "You can help folks get a good start in life by loaning them money to start a business. Banks won't loan colored folks a dime, so that's what the numbers man does, makes sure our colored community will not just survive but thrive."

Miss Josephine leans in and hugs him tightly. "One more question for you: do you remember the feeling you had when you played your first number 321 and won?"

"Do I? "DB asks excitedly. "Felt like I was on top of the world, that anything was possible." Miss Josephine replies, "That is the feeling that colored folks get when they hit a number. No matter how small, it gives them hope, they start to feel that despite all of the obstacles, there is a way to make it."

Again, Miss Josephine looks at DB. "How do you think Rev. Baker will feel about you choosing this life? How about your mother?"

"Mama has long suspected you're teaching me about the numbers. The word in the neighborhood is that you have had a numbers business since your husband died, took over for him. Mama likes a good life and will support me; she just would want me to stay safe." He shrugs. "Papa will get his preacher; Edward's following him to the pulpit."

"Your mother should have no worries; Miss Josephine knows everyone and everything necessary to keep you safe in this business. You just have to trust me, my directions, and the people who will be guiding you all the while. Do you want to join Miss Josephine in this venture?"

DB was half sure he was ready and half wanting to run out of the house, but with no more time to think about it, he blurted out, "Miss Josephine, I am ready to be my brother's keeper. Teach me everything you know. We didn't come all this way to Detroit to live like we had to in and the Greenwood in the South."

A few months later, at 16 years old, three months after his father dies, DB not only takes over managing the

Florida Market for his mother but starts collecting numbers for Miss Josephine. His heart swells with pride, he may not have become the preacher his father wanted him to become, to save souls and make colored folks comfortable in heaven, he will do it right here on earth, in Black Bottom.

Afterall, Papa gets his preacher -- Edward is already in the pulpit.

Mother Mary

"Did I ever tell you guys about the first time Miss Josephine took me to see Sister Mary?"

"Yeah, tell us, you mean that root woman from Mississippi? She saved us," says Rabbit with a mischievous smile.

"Well, I prefer to think of her as a spiritual advisor, I depended on her advice," replies DB.

"Was it scary? How old were you? What happened?"

DB proceeded.

"I think I had been working for Miss Josephine about a year or so. She said there was someone she wanted me to meet. A very important person to her and who could be of help to me. I said okay. So, we go over to Mother Mary's house. I admit the first time, it was a little creepy, but I saw some folks coming out that I would have never suspected would be in there. They just kind of turned their heads and kept walking. She kept appointments."

A young girl, maybe about 16 years old, opens the door for us and shows us into this dark room. A tiny, very dark old lady, wearing a black dress buttoned all the way to the chin, is sitting at the table. Her hair is covered with a white scarf. On the table is a red candle, a deck of cards, and a Bible. Mother Mary motions for us to sit down in the two chairs facing her.

She bows her head lightly to Josephine and says, "Welcome, Daniel. Josephine has told me all about you and what a fine young man you are."

"Thank you," says a nervous me.

Mother Mary places her hand on the Bible, turns to a certain book, closes her eyes and says a prayer to herself. Miss Josephine closes her eyes, but I am too curious to miss anything. Then Mother Mary starts to tremble and speak strange words in a weird voice. I try to hide that I am frightened. Finally, the trembling stops and she speaks.

"Some hard times are about to befall our people," she warns. I think colored folks always have hard times. As if she is reading his mind, Mother Mary says. "Yes, but the whole country will have bad fortune, and you know the saying, if white folks catch a cold, colored will get pneumonia."

She fixes her gaze on me, and I hold it. "Daniel, why do you think Josephine brought you to see me today?"

I gulp. "I don't know, mam."

"Daniel, you are a very special young man with many talents. Because of the gifts that God has given you,

you are chosen to help your people during these trying times." She pauses, closes her eyes briefly and all of a sudden is looking at me again. "You will help them by any means necessary. Sister Josephine will be your guide."

I gulp again, my heart is racing. "What is it that you want me to do? I will do anything to help my people."

Miss Josephine smiles broadly and says to Mother Mary, "I told you he was a very special young man."

"Sister Josephine says you are really a help to her since she has gotten older. You are now writing and picking up the numbers for her."

"Yes, mam."

"I help Sister Josephine by protecting her from any trouble with the police or anyone else who sells numbers. In fact, I help any numbers man or woman who has the sense to come to me."

"What kind of protection?" I ask warily.

"You realize that you could be in danger if the police ever caught you with your book or number slips on you?"

"Mam, I didn't think anybody but colored folks played the numbers."

"Well, ever since that big colored numbers man got kidnapped in Harlem, the white folks have begun to take notice of how colored folks are spending money. They say it's illegal to play the numbers even though we know white folks bet on the horses and there are after-hours gambling spots all over Detroit."

Mother Mary then reaches in her pocket and pulls out a little red flannel bag and places it in front of me. I'm getting more curious and more anxious.

"This is your mojo bag, son. It is filled with everything necessary to protect you. The only thing I need is a little bit of your hair and fingernail clippings."

This weirds me out and I unconsciously drop my hands off the armrests into my lap.

Mother Mary reaches again into her pocket, a small pair of scissors in her hand when she says to me, "Come around here please and kneel right down by me."

I look over at Miss Josephine. She nods. So, up I get and do as I'm told, no choice in the matter as far as I can figure.

Mother Mary takes my left hand and clips my four finger nails, then a little of the hair from the very top of my head. She places both in the bag. "You can go back now," she says.

I take a look at Miss Josephine who has an approving smile on her face.

With huge relief, I plop into my chair, my eyes on Mother Mary, wondering what I have to do next. She takes a brown root from the bag, and my anxiety returns. "See this?" She holds it up to me. "It is a High John the Conqueror root – it comes from the time our people was in slavery."

She gets up and comes back with another piece of the root, which she hands to me. "Keep this in your pocket. It will protect you from all harm. Keep this bag with you at all times also, and don't let anybody, under any circumstances touch it."

I nod my head that I understand, however much I don't. I want to ask her what happens to me if somebody grabs the root, but I don't have the nerve.

"Daniel, I have a piece of High John the Conqueror root in all the places where my numbers are written. It's hidden away. Most of the folks don't even know it is there. All of my writers and runners carry the root and the bag with them for protection. Son, I love you and I don't want anything to happen to you because you have a great responsibility that will soon be yours."

"You mean more than now??"

"Yes, son, but you will know in time."

Mother Mary counts thirteen cards from the top of a deck and spreads them on the table before me. "Turn over three of the cards, please." I hesitate and she says, "Just take a breath and choose at will." I take one from the middle and then one from each end. Both Mother Mary and Miss Josefine clap their hands and say "Thank you, God, for blessing this boy."

I am relieved they don't cry or say, 'Oh, no.' And I know I can't quit now.

"Let me tell you young man, why we are so happy," says Mother Mary as she looks at the first card. "This jack of clubs says you are a compassionate man with strong beliefs and high values."

I have a momentary pride at being called a man, but Mother Mary talks on, so I figure I'll have to dwell on that later.

"Miss Josephine saw how special you were many years ago. You are chosen to help our people."

Mother Mary turns over the third card. "The six of clubs! Wonderful! You will triumph in business; you will be very successful in all you do."

I try to squelch my bursting pride, knowing it's a big sin. Mother Mary saves me by continuing to talk as she studies the third card. "The ten of clubs says good fortune will come to you and yours, plus, a surprise is just around the corner waiting for you. You will come into unexpected good fortune that will enable you to carry out your work."

Miss Josephine grabs me and gives me a big hug. She takes my face in her hands. "Daniel, you are the only child I have ever known. My daughter died as an infant, then you came into my life. Thank you for being the son you have been to me and for now carrying on the work. I love you."

"Thank you, Miss Josephine. I love you too." I dare to ask, just so I might know what's going on, "What does it mean to carry on the work?" I find out exactly what she means some years later.

The Florida Wheel

DB opens the door and calls out to Miss Josephine as he has become accustomed to doing. A strange quietness is evident. No hum from the kitchen, no lights on, just silence. DB takes a look in the kitchen and calls to Miss Josephine again but no answer. His stomach sinks, and his breathing becomes rapid. For a moment, his mind is a total blank. He knocks gently on the partially open door to Miss Josephine's bedroom and calls to her again. No answer. He gently pushes the door. There she is still in the bed. He moves closer. Her eyes are closed, and her lips are curved into a slight smile. He is struck by the peaceful look on Miss Josephine's face. He calls her name softly again and then gently shakes her shoulder. No response. DB knows this is the moment that they had talked about but that he had feared, Miss Josephine is dead.

DB backs away from the bed, his eyes tightly closed and his hands drawn into tight fists. He stands there in the silence as tears flow down his cheeks. In his mind he hears Miss Josephine reminding him of his first task when she dies. He takes a deep breath and goes to her dresser. In the first drawer under her clothing is a white envelope. It reads, *To Daniel Austin Baker, Jr.* He slowly opens it.

"My dear son, if you are opening this letter, it means that the day we talked about has come. Miss Josephine has gone to the wide

beyond. You have become my son, my only living child. For that reason, everything that I own, I bequeath to you. Tom Carson, the lawyer, has a copy of my will, but in this envelope is a copy of the deed to this house, which I have deeded to you. This house and everything in it belong to you. I do ask that my clothing and other items that my people can use be given to them. Cora and Bell are about my size, have them come over and take the things that they would like to have.

Now for the most important thing, I give to you my numbers bank. Yes, Daniel, Miss Josephine had moved up in the numbers racket while you were helping me. I give to you all of my customers; they all know that when I am gone you will start your own wheel. Daniel, you are a good young man and I know that you will do well. There are some things that you must remember to have my blessings in this venture.

First, you are a businessman, not a gangster. Never let it be said that you used violence in any way. Colored numbers men are businessmen, not like white gangsters. You are never to lower yourself to the ways of the white gangs, like the Purple Gang. That does not mean that you should not have protection, because they will try to take over, especially during these trying times like they did in New York, but my sister Stephanie with the help of Bumpy Johnson was able to hold on. Find two to four good men to be your protection. Your friend rabbit loves you like a brother. He will be your loyal protector.

Second, our people are suffering in Detroit. They have been laid off from the plants, and if there is any work at all, it goes to whites, not colored. Whites are demanding that if a job is available, it goes to a white man. Half of all colored men here in Paradise Valley are unemployed. Your task is to hire as many of these unemployed men as possible, hire men first so that they can feel like men, that way they can pay their rent and buy food for the family. All around us, families are being thrown out of their apartments. Daniel, use the numbers to help our people. Hire them, pay them.

Third, Daniel be honest (which I know you will do because I know your upbringing and your character, your daddy did a good job even though you all sometimes disagreed). Pay all winning hits even if it breaks the bank. Your honesty will make the people love you. You will get the money back I assure you; my people believe in the power of the numbers.

Fourth, right now at this moment: Get the money out of the hem of every curtain in this room. Do it now, before you let anyone know that I am gone. You should find at least $6,000 in the curtains. With the $,4000 you have saved by working with me, you will have $10,000 to start a bank.

Fifth, consult often with Sister Mary. She will guide and protect you as she has me. Be sure to let her have what she would like from the house.

My blessings for the best of everything in life to you, my son. You will be a savior for the unemployed and those without hope here in Black Bottom and Paradise Valley. I love you dearly.

Momma Josephine

Inside of the envelope was the deed to the house, which he now owned. DB places the money inside the envelope, then goes next door to the neighbors to tell them that Josephine has died. The news spreads quickly through the neighborhood. On Saturday, DB's brother Edward, preaches Miss Josephine's funeral, for which DB pays. Afterward, he invites Miss Josephine's special friends, customers, and neighbors to the house for a repast and to get a token by which to remember her.

****

On Monday morning, DB gathered his family members, Rabbit, and his closest friends from Jackson County, Florida. His mother, who always favored Daniel, approved of his becoming a banker/businessman in Paradise Valley. His sister Susie would sell numbers from the family grocery that his father established, the Florida Market. His mother would have a writer at the flower shop next door. His sister Sally and her husband Robert at Barnes Funeral Home will be the location of the bank. Edward will use the church to launder the funds and establish a stationary shop that prints programs and other materials for churches in the city but also books for not only the Florida Wheel but all of the other wheels. DB sends for his Uncle George and his son to set up a barber shop as a front for writing numbers and his cousin Lucille to set up a beauty salon for the same purpose. Cousin Louise was the best cook in Greenwood, she was on the next train to establish the Florida Café. Rabbit will run a taxi and limousine service using the automobiles owned by the funeral home.

DB establishes a legitimate business as a real estate broker and insurance man. His cardinal rule is to own no business in which numbers were written or which served any type of alcohol or allowed any other forms of illegal gambling. He was a businessman and a provider for the people of Black Bottom and Paradise Valley through his numbers bank.

Darkness Then Light

Just four years after establishing the Florida Wheel, looming disaster appears. Detroit's economic environment had been good for colored because of jobs at the auto plant meant freedom from exploitive sharecropping in the South. Thousands had come to experience a new life in Detroit, but on Tuesday, October 29, the stock market crashed and doom fell like storm clouds upon Americans, especially its workers. Fifteen million Americans were unemployed and 60 percent of them were colored workers. Detroit was especially hard hit because of the losses suffered by the automobile industry. At the Ford Rouge plant, 60,000 Negroes were out of work. Life become totally uncertain for Detroit's colored population.

Rabbit bangs on DB's door and lets himself in. Rabbit's face is distorted by fear and anger. "Man, are you keeping up with the news? Do you know what is happenin'? Ford is letting our people go in droves. It like a fast-burning forest fire down there. They being fired right on the spot. The only folks they are keepin' are white folks and foreigners."

DB's shakes his head. "How can Ford do this after recruiting all these colored folks to come up here from down South to work for him?" He pushes his chair back, frustration all over his face. "White folks will look out for each other no matter, it's true, last hired and first fired."

"So, what are we going to do, DB? Our guys at Ford are back on the street. We gonna have a whole city of colored folks needin' work.

DB rubs his forehead, looks straight into Rabbit's eyes. "Rabbit, Mother Mary warned me of this in her last reading, said a darkness was going to fall over the country and especially Detroit. I didn't know what she meant, now I do. Guess we will have to do what Miss Josephine said. I must do as a numbers man, take care of my brothers. Rabbit, call a meeting right away, we'll do it at the funeral home and please let everyone know, no wheel this week." Rabbit rushed out of the office with a thumbs-up. DB started to reflect upon his life and this new development, nine years into the numbers racket, living a life of luxury, the bottom has collapsed. This will mean a new way of life for himself and his people.

The chapel at the funeral home is filled to capacity. Standing room only. Faces are wet with perspiration, eyes anxious, faces etched with fear. DB stands tall, clears his throat and begins to speak, looking each of his sixty workers in the eyes. "A catastrophe has hit this country, and Detroit in particular, Black Bottom will feel it the most. It has always been this way for our people, we have had to fight to survive. I know what it means to fight to make a way out of no way. From Cottondale, Florida, as a ten-year-old boy, we came to Detroit looking for a better life, just like I know all of you did. We colored people know how to survive, though." Amens are raised by the crowd. "We, all of us, including myself are going to regroup, develop a new plan for survival, looking out for all of our unemployed brothers and sisters as well. We all will make it work that we will eat and have a place to lay our heads."

The crowd applauds.

"Now, for the hard part, we will all have to take a cut in pay -- runners you will now get only a 15% commission because we have to hire at least 40 more of the unemployed colored to write. All you who were in the factories, try to find one or two men we can train. Also, we will add folks at all of our businesses – barber shops, stores. Sharing as a community is what the Florida wheel will help us do."

DB keeps his word, bringing in more writers and adding additional folks at all of his businesses. Colored folks from all professions seek work in the numbers racket. But there is a flicker of light, colored folks having so very little could only dream and believe that life could get better. Hitting the number is the way to bring financial relief. Colored people combine their few pennies to play the numbers. They buy dream books like mad; ministers give out numbers in scriptures, and hymn numbers are seen as possible hits. There is the reasonable chance that one small change could turn into a modest earning that puts food on the table or pays the rent. A one-dollar correct guess could bring $600, and the luckiest family in the Bottom put all their dollars together, and bet $25 on the week's winning number…which pays $10,000.

With winnings like that, word gets around, and the numbers racket takes off. It becomes the primary economic force during the 1930s in colored communities. Numbers men like DB seek respectability by investing gambling profits in legitimate businesses as well as sponsoring food giveaways, helping churches and organizations feed the poor, filling apartments with homeless families; it all comes from donations from the Florida Wheel. DB finds it almost hard to believe, but the darkness has turned to light, the '30s had makes him even richer. By 1932, he is bringing in $4000 a week, making him one of the richest men in Detroit, along with the original numbers Detroit kingpin John Roxborough, Bumpy Johnson in Harlem, and the Jones Brothers in Chicago.

October 27, 1934

"Man, They Are Killing Us"

DB, jolted awake by the ringing of the phone, shoots up like a canister fired from a canon, his heart thrusting against his chest. He lifts his hand to his moist face, the phone continuing to ring. Ruth, more asleep than awake, gives him a "what is it?" look and turns back over. Waves of fear envelope DB. Is this the phone call he dreads the most? He wonders if his worst nightmares have come to reality -- one of the runners has been careless and is arrested. The Wheel is being raided. He is afraid. Finally on the sixth ring, he slowly picks up the receiver and places it gently to his ear.

"Yelp, this is DB, what is it?" He is hoarse.

"Man, all hell has broken loose down here," the voice answers

"Down where? Who the hell is this?"

"Man, they are killing us." replies the desperate male voice.

"Killing who? Who is this?" DB shouts. Ruth turns over, wide awake.

"Man, it's your cousin Jacob. I know it's late, but this is the only time I could call, and we need your help desperately."

Relieved that it's not Rabbit or one of his other numbers men, DB takes a deep breath and lets out a loud sigh. He's finally figured out the voice. Ruth's eyes are questioning.

"Jacob, I'm sorry. This call, this time of the morning, ya know? Kinda unnerves a man. What's going on? Couldn't it wait until tomorrow?"

"DB, hell no, it couldn't wait. We are being killed." Jacob screams into the phone. DB moves the receiver away from his ear.

"What do you mean, 'killed'?"

"Colored folks in Marianna!" Jacob's cry is exasperated.

DB swallows, shakes his head as though none of this is making sense, but Jacob has his full attention now. "I am awake, talk to me."

"Yesterday, a gang of more than a thousand white folks tortured and hung Claude. They say it was terrible. Said he raped and killed the white girl that lived across the road from him. Carloads of them went 200 miles to Alabama to take him out of jail and bring him back to Greenwood to hang him."

"What? You don't mean Miss Smith's son?' Where are you? Are you okay?"

"I am calling from Miss Hunt's house, Mattie's boss lady. Her husband came and got me and they are keeping us here. Hidin' out in the woods or with white folks is the only way to be safe now.

"DB, white folks done gone crazy. After they tortured Claude, drug him behind a car and brought him to Marianna to hang on the courthouse lawn. Then they started grabbing up colored folks and beating them almost to death."

"Are they beating folks in Greenwood too? What about our family?" DB is getting angrier by the minute.

"All the colored folks in Greenwood is hiding out in the woods. Got their hunting rifles with them just in case, but you know they are outnumbered. But for now, it's just in town."

"What can I do? What do you need?"

"We needs to get outta here right away."

"I'll buy the tickets and have them wired. How many tickets do you need, children and all? I know you and Mattie and your kids, who else will leave?"

"Curtis, June and their kids. But man, as soon as I can get some word to the family, I will let you know. I just know we has got to leave here and soon."

"When will it be safe for you to go to Greenwood?"

"I'll ask Mr. Hunt to scout around for me. See when It's safe, and I'll let you know."

"Man, please be safe. I love you. I will do whatever is necessary to get you and the family out of there."

"Thanks, man. I will be in touch as soon as possible."

"Promise me, as soon as possible. I will be waiting by the phone." A sense of dread washes over him as he puts the receiver down.

"What is it, DB?" asks an anxious Ruth. "Who was that?"

"Cousin Jacob. He's hiding out with Mattie's white folks. Says they killed Claude, Miss Smith's boy, tortured and hung him."

Ruth lets out a mournful sigh.

"Now they are rounding up colored folks in Marianna, beating them."

"What about your family in Greenwood?"

"Says he thinks they're all hiding out for now or staying with white folks."

"DB, what're you going to do?"

"As soon as I know, I'll wire tickets to the railroad to get them out of there. I might as well get up and get some things moving. They won't be happy, but I've got to call Rabbit and the captains. Hell, I'll let Rabbit wake them up."

"What can I do to help?" asks Ruth.

"Get Susie over here, tell her you need her to make breakfast for the men. Get some coffee started until she gets here. Don't take no for an answer. If we ever needed her, it's now."

Ruth gets dressed. Knowing it's going to be a day full of people in her house, she puts her hair up as she hurries downstairs.

DB hits his hands against his forehead in exasperation, then dials Rabbit.

****

It's six o'clock in the morning. The Baker dining room is filled with a dozen or more men, including Edward and Rabbit. Susie has prepared a southern breakfast of bacon, sausage, grits, eggs and biscuits. DB lets them all dive in and finish before answering any of questions. They eat fast and anxiously wait. They do feel some sense of relief that this early morning meeting has nothing to do with the Florida Wheel, as DB says when they come in. They finish and DB invites them into his living room.

The men settle down on the lush brown leather sofas and chairs that fill the room. He brings in a few chairs from the dining room and has Susie place a coffee pot, cream, sugar, and cookies on tables around the room. All eyes are on DB. The men are restless, rubbing their pantlegs, talking to each other in low voices, letting out breaths audibly, looking around at one another.

He begins. "Everyone of us has our afterbirth buried under a tree in Greenwood, Cottondale, or Marianna. No matter how long we have been here, we go back yearly because we have family there." He takes a deep breath. All eyes on him, the men now with stretched necks are waiting for what he has to say; surely, he did not get them out of bed on a Saturday morning to reminisce about home.

He continues. "I got a call at 3 this morning from my cousin Jacob. He's hiding out with Mattie's boss man; he says colored folks in Marianna are being hunted down and beaten, maybe some have been killed." A collective sigh of horror fills the room. "Y'all know, or least most of you know Claude, Miss Smith's son. Seems they accused him of killing the white girl that lived across the road from him, tortured him in Greenwood and drug him behind a car all the way to Marianna where they hung him, right on the courthouse grounds."

"What?"

"Where was the sheriff?"

"Nobody did nothing?"

Then they began to answer their own questions. "You know ain't no white sheriff gonna stop that madness. He probably a member of the KKK hisself. "

"What's happening with our kinfolks in Greenwood and Cottondale?"

"As far as I know, they're hiding in the woods. I won't know any more until Jacob calls again."

"When you gonna hear from him? We need to know about our families."

"You can try to reach them but they all scared, hiding in the woods or with friendly white folks."

"So, DB, you called us here, what can we do?"

"Get some guns and go down there and kill crackers," comes a response from Nate, not known to take stuff from white folks. He escaped to Detroit because he killed a white man.

"No, Nate, you know we will be outnumbered. Drunk white folks will come from all over North Florida to kill niggas, especially if they see our out-of-state tags. We are just going to have to wait and see what Jacob reports."

Not to be deterred, Nate asks," Do we need to ship guns to them if we shouldn't go?"

"Hush, man, let DB talk."

"What I need from you right now is to find housing for our families. You know what Detroit is like. White folks here are not going to greet a bunch of colored folks fleeing the Klan with open arms, we got the Klan in full force right here. But go to every colored house on every street in Black Bottom and see who has rooms. I will see that old Jewish man who still has an apartment on the edge of Black Bottom and see if I can buy it. Scare him, tell him a bunch of colored folks are moving in and will tear up his place and maybe he ought to sell it to me and get out of the neighborhood while he can. "Laughter comes from the group.

"I don't know how many will come. But they will need money and jobs. We'll have to help them. They are our families. I will do all I can."

The men surround DB, pat him on the shoulder." We know you will."

"Well, as you know, the Wheel will be closed today." Moans come from the group. And complaining. "Really man?" But they know who's boss, and they quiet down.

"Yes, really. Let everyone know. We have a crisis on our hands. The Wheel will open when we know more from Marianna. Don't forget -- many people here have relatives in North Florida."

"That's why they are going to want to play, to win some money to help them."

"Sorry, Jack, no Wheel until I hear from Marianna." He looked at some of the disgruntled. "That's an order."

"Is that all?" asks Rabbit.

"Yeah, for now. Why don't you take a moment to get the captains organized for their tasks and then stick around so we can talk. Edward, I need to talk to you as well about how the church can help."

"Sure, brother, don't fret, God is on our side. He will protect our families. We just have to make sure they have a place when they get here."

"Did everybody hear what Rev. Baker said?" Rabbit shouted. "We have to take care of the Detroit end of things. Let's get organized by our areas." The reverend's eyes fill with worry, his face shows the stress and burdens of a colored man having seen this before. DB hugs him and goes upstairs to lie down.

Waiting...An eternity

DB lies down, but rest does not come. He shifts from side to side and his insides begin to feel like they're quivering. He watches the clock and the phone. He occasionally picks up the receiver to make sure the phone's working. Most disturbing are the images flooding his mind. He remembers from his childhood the orange sky that he thought was so beautiful, the shame when he was told what it was; the looks of farmer Green and his family as they enter the church.

Each time he closes his eyes, he sees parade of drunk and hateful white men surging past colored homes in Greenwood, all brandishing shotguns. His heart pounds, and he opens his eyes again.

Rabbit gives DB his report, each of the captains doing his duty to notify the customers that there would be no Wheel today, apprising them of the situation in Marianna, and seeking housing wherever they could. DB hugs his faithful top man and cousin. He suggests to Edward to ask for a collection to be taken tomorrow to aid the families of Marianna.

The day passes slowly. DB has no appetite, refuses to eat. He comes downstairs and sits in his favorite chair, but it gives him no comfort. His limbs tingle and his chest tightens as he obsesses over the call he's waiting for. By nightfall, DB's stomach is churning; after eating nothing all day, he retches and vomits bile. He becomes dizzy and lies down again. Ruth brings ginger tea to calm his stomach and chamomile tea to help him sleep. He drifts off after a while but is dogged by nightmares. He sees his cousin Jacob calling to him but is unable to get to a telephone as a mob springs up behind Jacob from the bushes, grabbing at him, a rope looped around Jacob's neck and pulled taut. The crowd of white men cheer as Jacob's body rises off of the ground. DB screams, "No, no, stop, that's my cousin, he's innocent!" Ruth rushes to his side to awaken him.

"DB, you're dreaming." She rubs his head, hugs him, "What is it, dear??"

DB shakes himself awake, sits up, grabs his wife. "I dreamed they hung Jacob and that's why I haven't heard from him."

"Oh, my darling, please be patient, try to think positively. You told me he was being protected by Mattie's white folks. Give him time to get back to you when he has news." She gently soothes his forehead. DB lies back with eyes closed for a moment, then peers at the clock and picks up the telephone receiver. All night the phone does not ring, and he cannot wait any longer. He places a call to Mattie's boss man, but no answer. Now he really starts to obsess. Maybe they too are killed or run out of town for helping Jacob and his wife.

DB feels like he's losing his mind. The thoughts of colored -- his relatives, and Jacob and Mattie, Curtis and June -- being chased by the white mobs: the women raped, the men beaten senseless, tortured, their private parts cut off and given out as souvenirs, and finally their tortured and already dead bodies swinging from a tree…. He sees houses burning; it's those living in Greenwood and Cottondale. The orange bowl of flames covers the sky. The images will not leave his mind no matter how hard he tries. His chest tightens and it became difficult to breath. He has to blow out short breaths to gain control of himself. He pants.

DB watches the clock, lifts the receiver, puts it back down, paces all night. When the sun comes up, an exhausted DB falls onto his leather sofa and weeps. Shortly after 10 on Monday morning, the phone rings and DB rushes to answer. It is Jacob.

"Are you alright? Why haven't I heard from you? I have been worried to death."

"DB, we need your help to leave, but the National Guard is here now, so we should be able to get on the train without getting shot. Mr. Hunt is going to take me to Greenwood today. I will call you as soon as I can to let you know how many adult and children's tickets we need. DB, you have no idea what this means to me and Mattie. Her white folks are good and want us to stay, but I have made her understand that we must leave. Colored folks will start to come home now that the National Guard is here. I will call you as soon as I can."

"Cuz, please call as soon as you know. I have aged 50 years in these two days; I can't even imagine what you've been through. Be careful. I love you."

DB is finally persuaded to eat a little dinner, Susie's macaroni and cheese and roast beef, his favorite. Ruth sits with him and assures him that all will be well. Both Rabbit and Edward stop by with good news -- temporary housing for as many as they could and more than $200 collected by the church.

The call from Jacob shortly after 6 p.m. tells the number of train tickets needed -- 56 people; forty adults and 16 children traveling to Detroit. DB goes to the Wheel Bank to get the money necessary to bring the families to Detroit. He makes an appointment with the Jewish owner of the apartment building to buy the building. He's successful in his negotiations.

Rabbit, who travels to Greenwood and Cottondale often to secure country meats and vegetables for the Florida market, comes up with a brilliant idea: have the families bring all the meat from their smoke houses, and all the vegetables they can sell at the market. This money will also be used to help them get settled. DB calls Jacob to ask Mr.

Hunt to see that the foods are shipped with the passengers, and that he will make it worth Mr. Hunt's while.

This is a weekend that DB and all his friends and family will never forget. He has used more money from the Wheel than he ever paid out for a big hit, but he remembers the words of Miss Josephine: "Numbers are for the liberation of colored people." DB has liberated 56 people from the racial terror of his home state. He can breathe easy now. When he gets word that the group has departed, he learns, sadly, that they were warned to leave or face the worst.

The Good Times

"Man, there were some very serious moments, but overall, the numbers racket provided good times," Rabbit says thoughtfully.

"Those were some of the best days of our young lives," agrees Edward.

"You two and the organization that helped to run it made it all possible," says DB.

"But you were our leader, and a great leader you were -- King of the Numbers Racket," laughs Rabbit. "Remember how you handled the "348" crisis when the bank was overrun? Every colored preacher must have preached from Psalm 34:8 that Sunday about taking their needs to God, 'cause every Negro playin' in Black Bottom played that number. It was crazy. DB, you paid every man and woman who hit the number, no holding back."

"Yeah, I had to borrow money from the market and thanks to the reverend here, the church. We were able to cover the bets and get back on our feet," agreed DB.

"Want to know what I think were some of our best times?" inquires Rabbit.

"No, which?" respond DB and Edward.

"Idlewild was the best investment that you made, DB. That's where all the top Negroes had land. Madame C.J. Walker, W.E.B. DuBois and that famous doctor from Chicago hung out there. Garveyism was quite visible in Idlewild. Remember when we gave that fundraiser for Garvey? Raised over $50,000 for him?"

"As I can remember," laughs Edward, "Idlewild was a favorite place for all the numbers kings to meet. The Jones Brothers from Chicago, and that crew from Cincinnati would be there every summer. "

"Yeah, that was a good investment, six two-story stone cottages set off from the lake, a beautiful view and rich Negroes lived like white folks there. Everything from fishing, hunting, horseback riding, camping and nightly entertainment. Rightfully so, it was called Idlewild the Black Eden" of Michigan."

"The stable and horseback riding camp we owned did very well, too," added DB.

"My great-grands still go there every summer and stay in the Baker compound," adds Edward

"Do you realize what we owned in Black Bottom and Paradise Valley during the good times? Everything from the funeral home, the Florida Market, the Florida Café, the cab company, auto repair shop, interest in barber and beauty shops, a drugstore, dress shop, and confectionary," responds Rabbit.

"Those were the days until they came to the very sudden and unexpected ending, but all in all, everything worked out for the best for us. No jail time and no violence from the white gangs," replied DB.

"Yeah, Rabbit, Robert and I as well as a bunch of others thought you had lost your mind. Frankly, I was quite angry, but DB, you knew how to listen and to act," confessed Edward. "Thank you for your good sense in that situation."

"I had to show my gratitude to Mother Mary, she never had another issue with money. Took care of her until the end and gave her the best funeral that an elder could have. She saved us."

The Warning

DB is catching up on paperwork regarding the inspection of his apartments and rooming houses, when the young man knocks on his office door. "Hello, Mr. Baker, Mother Mary sent me."

"Okay, come in, what is it?" inquires DB. "Is Mother Mary, okay?"

"Yes sir," replies the young man, "but she says she needs to see you right away; you must come with me now."

DB feels his chest tighten as he grabs his keys and heads out the door. Thoughts race through his head. What could be so wrong that Mother Mary insists I come to see her now, without an appointment?

DB reaches Mother Mary's apartment and she greets him at the door. "Come in, my son." Her usually calm demeanor appears to DB to be pure anxiety. "Please sit down. I had a premonition last night; Josephine came to me in a dream and asked me to give you a warning."

"Warning about what?" inquires a now profusely sweating DB. "There are forces that are your enemies and will be coming to destroy your business."

"What forces?" asks an impatient DB.

"The police and the mob."

"But I have paid for police protection for years and the mob has never come after me, I stay in my territory."

"But the police are after the colored numbers racket now and the mob plans to take over since there is no longer a prohibition on whiskey. They want some of what they call "nigger pennies."

DB takes a deep breath. "I can't believe this is happening. Are you sure, Mother Mary?"

"Let us see what the cards say; we will follow whatever comes up, because it is your spirit directing the cards that you choose."

Mother Mary anoints DB's forehead with holy oil and asks him to shuffle the deck of cards and divide the deck into three portions. She then asks him to pull one card from each of the three piles.

DB pulls the first card. "This is the Five of Swords, it says I will face conflict, hostility and tension. I will lose in the big picture, right now, move on. 'Let go' is the advice, reads DB.

His body is shaking. He can barely catch his breath.

"Go on," she says.

He pulls the second card. "This is the Fire of Wands. It also warns of conflict, competition, not being able to find harmony or common ground with enemies, it shows me in the midst of battle."

He quickly pulls the third card. "Go on with the bad news," he grunts.

"This is the Tower, it shows danger, crisis, sudden change, upheaval, chaos but higher learning and liberation. DB, remember that even in times of disaster, there is always Divine Intervention. He holds his head in his hands, shaking it in total disbelief that this is the message he is receiving.

Mother Mary says it. "You must shut down the numbers wheel immediately to save yourself and your workers from jail or violence and the loss of all of the assets you have worked so hard to attain, even the legitimate ones."

DB's heart is pounding, eyes bulging, insides feeling that they are going to explode. "How long do I have?" he asks.

Mother Mary closes her eyes, chants for a few minutes, then says, "The last wheel must be Friday and Saturday, no more. Today is Monday, you have only a few days to get everything in order," she warns.

DB, almost speechless, shivering all over, thanks Mother Mary and races to this office. He immediately contacts Rabbit, Edward, and Sally's husband, Robert, his second in command. They all hear the urgency in DB's voice and rush over.

When they arrive, they see a DB they haven't seen or recognized since Billy's murder. He is rocking in place, his head in his hands. "DB, what is it?" they all ask at once.

"Our business is over, we must close down the last wheel on Saturday, there is danger for us. I just left Mother Mary's. She sent a messenger for me to see her so she could warn me."

"But DB, is she sure? How does she know this? She's an old lady, a root woman, can you believe this? Does she want money or something?" inquires a disbelieving Robert.

"Yeah, how do you know this is real?" asks Edward. Rabbit shakes his head in skepticism.

DB glares at Edward and angrily replies, "Mother Mary has protected us all of these years, you never doubted her before, why now? She is guided by our ancestors, Miss Josephine came to her in a dream and told her to warn me, then I pulled the cards from the deck myself with the same warning. We must listen to her," DB says at the end of his tirade, very quietly, very disconcerting to his men.. He is angrier than they've ever seen.

Edward, Robert and Rabbit, now sweating profusely, and breathing heavily, stare into space, unnerved by DB's intensity. Despite this, his brother Edward the preacher surprisingly asks sarcastically, "Then what now, if we are forced to shut down operations because of Mother Mary's message?'

"We must call all workers in; I mean everybody. For a meeting this evening at the funeral home. It is mandatory that everyone attend. Anyone not attending will be fired," says DB, his voice fading off, his head now down.

The writers, runners, checkers, every level of the business squeeze into the funeral chapel. Their eyes wide with anxiety, they wait, edgy about why they're summoned. The last time they were called to a meeting like this was the bad news of the depression.

DB wipes his brow, takes a deep breath, looks into the eyes of the crowd. "I have bad news, as you probably imagined. I have been given a warning. The Florida Wheel must close on Saturday And be no more."

Cries of "What?" "What is going on?" What are you saying, man?" "Are you serious?"

DB lets them wind down. "I know this is quite a shock. It was to me, to all of us who heard the news earlier this afternoon."

"But why? What did we do? We are always careful, follow all the rules. How do we live now?" roars the crowd, some standing and waving arms furiously.

"Please sit and listen. I am feeling just like you, the Florida Wheel has been my life for the last 25 years, my passion and my joy. But forces, enemies, are actively trying to bring the Florida Wheel down. Unless we want to face prison, or violence by the white mobs, we must shut down immediately."

The crowd roars back. "We can fight the Tally's and any other cracker that wants to take our business. Is it Roxborough and some other Negroes or the crackers that you're worried about?"

"It is first the police, who will now turn on us, and then the mobs, who are our enemies. We have paid all bribes to the cops but apparently not as much as the white mobs will now pay them. We have never had trouble with the colored kings because we have always stayed in our territory."

"So, are the other colored numbers closing down or just us? Why us?" Again, the crowd.

"We have creditable evidence that we must close now. Don't worry about anyone else's business, we must take care of ourselves. We must let all of our customers know immediately that the last wheels will be on Friday and Saturday. The results will be shared in all the shops, payouts immediately given. After Saturday, all banks and anything and everything that has to do with the numbers in your possession must be brought to the funeral home on Saturday so that it can be destroyed. There can be nothing on your person, in your home or anywhere that connects you to the numbers racket after Saturday."

They argue and yell and punch the air. Their faces are angry, stunned, afraid.

DB let them, for a while, then continued. "Brothers and sisters, we will survive this. Remember just a few years back during the dark days of the depression, we made money, all of us did even better than before. Every man and woman who now works in the numbers will have employment in our legitimate businesses, we will even help those of you who want to start a business of your own to do so. We together as the Florida Wheel will survive. Please trust me. Have I ever let you down?"

The crowd shakes their heads in a negative response to the question. Heads down, some teary-eyed, they leave in silence.

The loss of the Florida Wheel could be felt on the streets, in shops, there was a sense of sadness, even depression. The hope of achieving a colored man's American dream was disappearing. Sure, there were other wheels, but the Florida Wheel. was special. What occurred on Friday and Saturday was shocking and amazing. Colored folks played numbers like there was no tomorrow, families put money together to bet on a number, played more than one number straight and in combination, some played they entire paychecks for the week. There was not a dream book left on shelves, and preachers were praying and giving out scriptures to read all week long. On the last day of the wheel, $25,000 had been bet, the largest betting in the history of the Florida wheel. DB, Robert, Edward, and Rabbit tried not to act overwhelmed.

After payouts were made to a few winners, severance pay was given to all employees. Through the weeks ahead, full-time writers, runners, and checkers were placed in legitimate businesses. The only holdover from the Florida Wheel was a special day once a month when a Florida favorite, "Bolita," the Cuban game, was played in barber and beauty shops with a select group of customers, which provided a small hope of winning something.

The 1941 headlines in the Detroit News bolted DB from his chair. "John Roxborough and others are being tried for an extensive numbers racket in Detroit." It had been less than a year since DB closed the Florida Wheel. Edward, Robert, and Rabbit had to admit that DB had been right to follow the advice of Mother Mary and the ancestors.

Things ended well for DB and the Florida Wheel. The legitimate businesses brought in huge profits. It was only after the 1967 rebellion that DB decided to leave Detroit, like the white folks, and move back to Florida. They spent the last 30 years running a cattle farm, funeral home, liquor store, and restaurants in Cottondale, Greenwood, and Marianna, until the great-grands decided it was time for the trio to truly retire.

The Most Bitter Memory

"Bro, it's four o'clock in the morning, like we got out of Detroit and Cottondale, it is time for us to get out of here and get some sleep' enough of the memories for old men, time to get some rest" says a yawning Rabbit. Edward agrees and they both go to the guest room.

The trio has Iy avoided the most painful memory of their days in Detroit. DB, knows however, that the story of his life in Detroit is not complete without the most bitter memory. He remembers and relives every moment of that fateful evening.

December 24, 1935

Adams is blocked as valets scurry to park a bevy of the latest model automobiles driven by chauffeurs of the crowd of well-dressed Negroes entering the 666 Theatre Cabaret. Mink covered women in sparkling jewels laugh and chat gleefully as they enter the establishment.

DB has rented Detroit's finest night club and cabaret for a Christmas party and celebration in honor of his brother, William (Billy) Frederick Douglas Baker is graduating from Wilberforce University in the coming spring session. Over 200 people have been invited to attend the season's most socially-defining affair. Members of

Detroit's elite as well as from Policy (numbers racket) Kings and Queens from Chicago and Harlem.

The guests enter a room with a Cotton Club atmosphere. The energy is the room is electric as guests find their way to the bar trimmed in green and gold Christmas lights, and candle-lit tables covered by green satin table cloths. Waiters dressed formally in white jackets and black trousers, serve carved turkey, ham, and roast beef. Platers of chilled shrimp and lobster tails as well as salads of all sorts are spread on buffet tables. A dessert table is filled with delicacies of southern desserts such as coconut cake and sweet potato pies.

The famous McKinney's Cotton Pickers band is playing favorites like Cab Calloway's "Minnie the Moocher". Suddenly, a chorus of light-skinned dancing girls appear, wearing skimpy gold-trimmed green satin outfits, gold feathered headdresses, and gold shoes. Their outfits were especially chosen to match the green and gold school colors of Wilberforce College.

A large Wilberforce banner hangs from the ceiling. Wilberforce College was founded in 1856, before the Civil War and was a destination point for the Underground Railroad. The AME church affiliated college was named after 18th century abolitionist William Wilberforce and was the first college owned and operated by African Americans.

DB taps on his champagne glass and asks the guests to toast William "Billy" Baker.

"This is a very special event for the Baker family, my beloved baby brother Billy as we all know him will be the third Baker and second generation to graduate from Wilberforce, the college attended by my father Daniel Baker, Sr., and my brother, Rev. Edward Baker. I am the slacker of the family." Everybody laughs; everyone in the room knows that at only 25 years of age, DB became millionaire." Billy is the bright and shining hope, the dream of the Baker family, he will reach heights that none of the Baker boys or girls before him has ever reached. He has no struggles only the future before him. My father, the Rev. Daniel Baker Sr., left the state of Florida, and came to Detroit so that his family, so that Billy would be the dream. When my father died, I promised him that Billy would become the scion of this wonderful Baker family one day. Not fortunate enough to have children of our own, Billy has become my son rather than just a brother. Family is all there is for we Bakers, followed of course by our community. It is the role of every Baker to use his or her gifts and talents in service to our Detroit community. Billy will carry on this practice when he graduates from Wilberforce and God knows where else to start the Baker Family Trust to provide for the dreams of boys and girls from Black Bottom and Paradise Valley. Whether they want to become a doctor, lawyer, teacher, preacher, or business owner, the Baker Foundation will assist them to achieve their dreams. Now let's raise our glasses in a toast to Billy Baker." Everyone raises glasses and salutes Billy. "Speech, speech," the crowd yells. Billy, tall, handsome in his tucks, with light-brown skin, hazel eyes, wavy black hair, a narrow nose and lips, a dazzling smile and soft voice joins DB.

Billy speaks. "I am overwhelmed. I never expected this type of honor. I want to thank my dear brother DB, for his wisdom and guidance through the years." He hugs DB. "DB I will not let you, the family, or this community down," he says looking out at the audience. "Before you go have a couple of gifts for you. His mother Lillian, siblings, Edward, Susie and Sallie join DB and Billy. Billy's mother, presents him with a set of keys to a 1935 Chevy Coop, a gift from the family. "The family wants you to enjoy your last semester at Wilberforce in style," she says as she hugs Billy. Billy hugs all of his siblings. "Now, this is from big brother DB to remind you of this night and your responsibility to give back to this community." From a small velvet bag, DB pulls out a ring, an emerald surrounded by raised letters spelling, WILBERFORCE COLLEGE. He places it on Billy's right ring finger. "Wear this proudly and know how much pride you family takes in you and in what you will accomplish. You are the fulfillment of the dreams of this family and your ancestors." Tears fill Billy's eyes, those of the family, and many in the audience. "Okay, folks, enough for the sentimentality, lets jive a little, Cotton Pickers, let us have it.

Get on the dance floor and show your stuff. They call y'all "elights" but tonight let's "delight". The crowd laughs voraciously and heads to the dance floor. Billy and his longtime girlfriend, Alice, dressed in gold lame head for the dance floor.

****

As DB finally slips into bed, tears flood his eyes. He has achieved everything that he has desired in his 100 years, except the most important thing. For the last 75 years are more he has searched for the man or men who murdered his baby brother William or Billy to him. He has vowed to find and kill the murderers. There is no real joy for DB tonight, perhaps with the exception of seeing his family members, but the great-grand twins look uncannily like their great-uncle that his sadness returns. Tonight, he weeps uncontrollably as he did 75 years ago. In 75 years, not a day has passed that he has not thought of his vow to catch and kill the man or men responsible for this reprehensible act. He plays scenes from the day he got the news over and over in his head. He says to himself, "What if? Why didn't I take the money and gifts to Maude? Why was I so self-absorbed? Why had I cheated on my wife that night with a show girl for heaven's sake? "DB had always carried a loaded gun in his ankle holster, Billy never did. If he had a weapon, even if he died, he could have killed at least one of them and perhaps still been alive. He would not have been defenseless.

"How stupid was it of me to let Billy go alone that night? Why hadn't I sent one of my men with him. Here I am 100 years old, living in a retirement home. What chance will I ever have to fulfill my promise to Billy?" DB buries his face into his pillow and as he does almost every night now. Two heart attacks in the last three years, he knows that few years are promised him now and he that he might die before he gets the revenge he seeks.

As he done when the feelings of grief and anger overtake him, DB goes to the special drawer in which he keeps all of the reminders of his life. He pulls out a folder marked "Billy's Murder- December 26, 1935. The first dreadful news appeared on page 2 of the *Detroit Courier*.

December 26, 1935

The Detroit Courier (page 2)

The unidentified barely clothed body of a Negro male was found in a field near 10-mile road. The body clad only in tee shirt and undershorts, and without shoes or socks was found by teenagers playing in the field. The victim had one gunshot wound to the head and five to his upper body. The body has been identified as that of William Frederick

Douglas Baker, a member of the prominent Negro Baker family here in Detroit. Baker's car was found abandoned and vandalized on December 24, and the family reported him missing on Christmas morning. The Detroit Police are investigating but have no clue as to how long the body has been here or what was the motivation for the killing. If anyone has any information regarding this crime, please contact the Detroit Department.

 The report does not report the victim wearing a ring. Underneath the first article lies the most crucial information. DB's grief turns to rage as he reads it. On the top page is the article about the Black Legion. He removes the article and reads it for the thousandth time.

The Detroit Courier- Page 1

A secret society that practices ritual murder, and is known as the Black Legion, has been discovered in Detroit. A number of its members are to be charged with murder. It is believed by the police to be an offshoot of the Ku Klux Klan and to have more than 10,000 members. The Black Legion, an offshoot of the Ku Klux Klan, is a militia group and white supremacist organization in the midwestern United States. The Black Legion is operating during the Great Depression of the 1930s. Detroit had been a strong center of KKK activity in the 1920s, and in 1931, a chapter of the Black

Legion formed in Highland Park, Michigan, by Arthur F. Lupp, Sr. The Black Legion operates in gangs brutalizing, committing arson, and murdering as a way to enforce their idea of what America should be or look like. Since 1933, they are rumored to be responsible as many as 50 unsolved murders. A tearful and angry Daniel Baker, brother of slain William Baker insisted that the police continue to search for the evidence to convict the murderers of his brother.

DB places the news articles back in the folder and climbs into bed. His heart is heavy with grief and guilt. He has spent thousands of dollars and years of searching for the men. DB had read of Walter White's exploits in infiltrating the KKK in the South. DB enlisted the help of his "light, bright and almost white" cousin Alvin and paid him a good price to pretend to be white and become a member of the Black Legion. His efforts paid off. Alvin had heard the brags of the three men who killed the "smart-ass in your face nigga", had it coming to him", they laughed. Alvin got the names and reported to DB, for his safety, Alvin then left to live in Jamaica. DB put spies in every automobile plant and any other industry that would hire colored to find the three men, Earl Lee, and his nephews Roy and Ray Moses Lee, but to no avail. Finally, he gave up the search.

DB has asked only one prayer of God, to find and punish the men who murdered his brother. Today, he says the same prayer. "Father, I know that I have not always been an obedient servant, I have sinned against your commandments, but you are a good God and I am told you will forgive me my trespasses as I have to forgive others. But God, in all of your mercy I ask you at the dusk of my life to grant my one prayer, to find and punish those you killed my beloved Billy. Father, I will accept eternal damnation in hell, if you will only grant this one prayer. I do not have many years left, please hear me, I thank you for answered prayer. I believe you will hear my cry. Amen." As tears flow down his cheeks, DB finds some solace in his prayer of surrender to God. He has spent thousands of dollars and years searching for the men but to no avail. Now at 100 years old, he surrenders to God, even as his preacher father would say accepting eternity in the fires of hell. For DB, it will all be worth it; nothing could be worse that every day of the last seventy-five years of his life spent in hopelessness.

Book II

Justice

The Ring

The pale spiderweb-like blue veined hand rests lightly upon the back of the chair. He moves the hand slightly as the line inches slowly toward the bar to get drinks. As DB casually looks down at the ring on the man's hand, his skin begins to tingle, heart starts to race, eyes bulge, and his mouth stands agape. He shakes his head and slaps his right eye, but the small engraved letters that circle the emerald seem to jump out at dizzying speed and flash before his face; W I L B E R F O R C E COLLEGE. DB squeezes his eyes shut and when he opens them, he is blinded by the letters. Shaking his head, he keeps saying to himself, "It can't be, no it can't be," but he realizes this is the ring.

Breathless and shaking, DB tries to grasp the finger, but the hand is moved away as the man moves forward in the line. DB cannot believe what was happening to him, the letters are surrounding him, circling his head, WILBERFORCE COLLEGE. He tries to grasp the letters as they dance around his head. He feels a sense of euphoria, even giddiness as he reaches out to touch the letters. Suddenly, he begins to struggle for air, he clutches his chest, his body begins shaking violently, his knees fold, and he collapses.

The crowd begins to scream and the receptionist, Irene, rushes over, pushes the crowd back. She grabs a pillow from one of the sofas, places DB's head upon it, and loosens his shirt. A staff member quickly calls 911. Irene in her comforting voice keeps telling DB, "You will be just fine Mr. Baker, help is on the way. The EMT soon arrives, gives DB oxygen, takes his vitals, and prepares him to go to the hospital.

DB goes in and out of consciousness. When he wakes, he struggles to reach the letters that still dance around his head. Don't worry Mr. Baker, you will be fine," the attendant assures him. "No, but the letters, they are on the ring, I have to catch them," he insists. The attendant gently rubs his forehead and gives him a sedative.

Miracle

DB awakes to look into the sad, bloodshot eyes of two old white-haired men looking down on him. Tears stream down the faces of Edward, and Rabbit as DB opens his eyes. DB tries to speak. They lean in closely to his face to hear what he was saying. Slowly and painfully DB speaks.

"It's a miracle."

Edward put his hand up to his mouth, "Yes, a miracle."

"You are right man; we were mighty afraid for you. This was your third heart attack."

Ignoring what Rabbit just said, DB again whispers, "It's a miracle."

"I know man, you are right," says Rabbit.

DB shakes his head slowly side to side indicating "no". "I mean the …. ring".

"The ring? What ring" ask Rabbit as he and Edward now frown with questioning looks.

"What are you talking about Bro?" asks Edward.

"I found the ring." DB says with great effort and then closes his eyes.

"Do you think he hit his head when he fell or had a stroke too that has affected his brain? asks a bewildered Rabbit wild-eyed with a gaping mouth."

"Naw, man it was just a heart attack. May be is just a little confused with all of the medication and stuff."

DB opens his eyes and reaches up to grab Rabbit's hand, he firmly holds on to his right ring finger. "I saw the ring on his finger." He says breathlessly.

"Talk to me DB, whose finger and what ring?".

"Billy's ring? "Both men question with wide eyes and gaping mouths.

"Man, it's been over eighty years since anybody seen that ring do you know how many pawn shops we checked in Detroit and nothing." Rabbit says with a frown and deliberate tone.

DB just shakes his head and closes his eyes.

"How could he think he saw Billy's ring?" asked to Edward, ignoring DB.

"Don't be so hard on him, you know he has suffered and grieved for years for Billy."

"Well, seems like every time that ring comes up, seems like DB has a heart attack. Edward…" Rabbit says his name firmly, "remember the last heart attack, when we thought we had tracked the killers down, but it turned out to be the wrong men. DB couldn't take it. Here we are again, a third heart attack, I thought he made a promise then that he was leaving this behind him long ago."

"Yeh, poor Bro has outlived his wife. He doesn't even mention her anymore, but don't seem like he will ever forget Billy."

"He ain't never let go of that feeling of guilt, that he could have done something different, but it ain't his fault. Billy disobeyed and went where he knew colored folks should never be. He knew what the other side of Woodward was like for colored, better not get caught there. I just don't see why DB won't let this go."

DB opens his anger filled eyes. He glares at one then the other man. How dare they talk as if he isn't in the room? Have they no respect?

"DB, we didn't mean nothin' man, we just worried about you" apologizes Rabbit.

Edward reaches down to kiss DB on the forehead, and he turns away. Tears fill Edward's eyes. The two old men take their usual places at chairs in DB's room, but he refuses to open his eyes. He only acknowledges the hospital staff. At this moment, Edward and Rabbit are dead to DB. He whispers orders to the nurse that he does not want any visitors.

Without the intrusion of Edward and Rabbit, DB settles into only himself. He starts from the day the family left Cottondale, Florida and migrated to Detroit. Each day, after his luncheon meal, he asks for a glass of ice water, and draws into memory another chapter of his amazing life from migrant to millionaire.

It's Not Dementia

Daniel Austin Baker, Jr., has been in charge of everybody and everything concerning him for almost 80 years. Two weeks ago, he turned 100 years old. His temperament is noticeably different; he is irritated with the two men closest to him. He cannot believe that his own sibling and his top lieutenant and closest friend for 50 years are now doubting his judgment. Since he was 20 years of age and entered the Policy game, his judgment or decisions have never been questioned.

After three weeks at the Rehabilitation Center, DB is able to come back to his apartment. He however, hardly speaks to Edward, and completely ignores Rabbit when he comes to visit. He does not go down for meals with them but has his delivered to the apartment. Edward and Rabbit sit on the lanai with their bottle of Crown Royal but without the company of DB.

Finally, Rabbit has had enough.

"DB, what is the problem man? You act like you hate us or something."

Glaring and with pursed lips, DB responds. "No, I don't hate either of you, but I am very disappointed that you would believe I am losing it. Edward is younger than me and remembers far less than I do. How dare the two of you think that I have dementia."

"DB, we didn't say such a thing."

"Yes, you did, "DB yells. "You thought I was asleep in ICU and I heard you talking about my hitting my head or having a stroke. I am fine. I have complete control of my senses. "

"Bro, can't we all just get along?"

"Yeh, Rodney King. Do I need the shit beat out of me too?" DB asks with a smirk.

"All we have, we need each other," Edward says with tears in his eyes.

"I did see the ring," says DB gritting his teeth. It is not dementia. I will find the man wearing Billy's ring, whether the two of you help me or not."

"Okay, we believe you," insists Rabbit. "How can we help?"

"Be on the lookout. Look at the right hand of every white man you see in this complex. Be nosy, make friends. Shake hands. The ring is on the finger of a man who lives here."

"Okay, boss, we've got it. Why don't we start by getting down to dinner early? Maybe the buffet so we can see more people."

"Sounds like a plan to me," says Edward as he gives DB a big hug. DB however doubts what good the two will do, Edward can't remember or hear a damn thing, needs a scooter to get around, and Rabbit is totally stubborn and hot-headed at times.

DB Has an Idea

The trio takes the elevator up to the dining room on the second floor. They sign in and are shown to their table. A young Jamaican male with whom they are friendly struts over to wait on them. DB has a flash of an idea as the young fellow approaches. His eyes light up and he grins like a man with a secret.

"Hello, my favorite gentlemen, how are you this evening? And Mr. Baker, I am so happy to see that you are able to join us in the dining room again."

They all nod hello.

"Young man," begins DB with a broad smile on his face. "Come a little closer, I have something to ask you."

The young man places his ear against DB's face.

"Do you think you would be able to identify a Negro who is passing for white?"

The waiter steps back, frowning. "Well, I guess so, I don't really make it a habit of trying to identify someone's race."

"Well, this is somewhat special and will be worth your while."

The waiter looks around the dining room and leans in closer. "I notice a white man wearing a ring that is from a Negro college. At his age, he would have had to be black to have attended there, with segregation and all. I am just curious, and if he is black, I would like to make his acquaintance." He looks around again and then to DB says, "Well, what do you want me to do?"

"Simply observe. The man in question is wearing a gold ring on his right hand with an emerald in the center, and with the words "Wilberforce College" surrounding the stone. This is simply my curiosity. By the way, did you ever read the book "Passing" by Lena Larson? It's a great book."

"No sir, I haven't."

"I will get it for you. But do you understand? Just an old black man remembering the days when black folks who could passed for white did so. In my day, we used to play a game of spotting those with our features who were passing. Just humor me, young man, and like I said, if you can find him, there will be a reward for you."

"So, you just want me to see if I can find the guy wearing the ring you described?"

"That's right, and give me his name, so I can check out some old college year books. My brother went to Wilberforce."

"Can't you just ask him if he knows the guy?"

"It's not that easy, that brother died years ago."

"I'm sorry, sir. Okay, I will get to it for you. Now what would you like to drink?"

The trio devise a plan to scope out the entire community to find the mystery man wearing the ring. Each snoops around by joining new activities and making friends. They definitely go to all social hours.

The Wearer of the Ring

Winston Smith, the 19-year-old waiter of Jamaican descent, eagerly awaits DB, Edward, and Rabbit's arrival for dinner. He races toward them, eyes wide and aglow, almost out of breath. He wants to be the one to seat them tonight, he is so anxious that he even forgets to bring the menus.

He seats them as far away from the other diners as he can.

"Forgive me, in my excitement, I forgot to bring the menus." He returns with the menus and three glasses of water. With raised eyebrows, DB asks, " Do you have something for me?"

"Yes, sir, took a while, but I have all that you asked for right here." Winston slips a paper into the menu that he gives DB, who slowly opens the note. He lets out a big sigh and reads: *Earl Lee is the wearer of the ring. The other two are Ray Moses Lee and Roy Lee; they eat every meal with him. I don 't think he is passing. He sounds like a southern white man to me. Let me know if you need more.* A broad smile covers DB's face, he even lets out a hearty laugh as he passes the note to Edward. Smiles spread over their faces as they read.

"Should I give you gentlemen a few more minutes before you order?"

"Yes, please," says Rabbit. Winston leaves and returns a few minutes later. DB has a $100 bill folded in his pocket.

"I think we will all have the buffet," says DB. He opens his hand slightly so that Winston can view the bill. Winston's eyes widen. DB pretends to drop his napkin, and nods for Winston to kneel down to pick it up. DB slips the bill into Winston's pocket as he hands over the napkin.

"Thank you, sir," says Winston. DB lifts his finger to his lips. Waiters at Palm Haven are forbidden to get tips of any kind. In fact, they can be fired for taking tips. At Christmas, all of the resident's chip in to give all employees a Christmas bonus.

"Thank you, Winston, for directing us to the buffet tonight. I think I will take my soup to eat later," says DB.

"And you Mr. Baker, and you Mr. Edwards, would you like to take your soup home tonight as well?" Edward nods yes, and Rabbit, not hearing, just follows Edward's lead.

The trio is so excited they almost dance over to the buffet. Many watch them, talking among themselves, relieved that these three well-liked black men are so cheerful; they have seemed glum for too long.

One of their friends remarks as they pass, " You must really enjoy this meal."

"You have no idea," proclaims DB.

The trio eventually leaves for their after-dinner drink in DB's apartment.

Rabbit

The despair that hung over DB seemed even greater now…one of the men who had tortured and murdered Billy was now dead, but just hearing the words of Billy's last minutes sent DB further into despair. Perhaps revenge would not heal the womb. Rabbit loved DB like a brother, his respect and loyalty to the man had no bounds. He had pledged his allegiance to DB in any way possible since the day he had bumped in to him at the Florida Market.

****

Scrappy as he was, he had been reduced to a starving refugee from far away Cottonwood, Florida. He was heading toward a grocery called Florida Market, and he didn't know if he was going to ask for a job or steal something to eat.

Until somebody bumped into him, which startled him. Could people tell what he was thinking? He looked up and relaxed a little – he knew who it was, but it took the man a minute. Then,

"Man, look at you," said a surprised DB. "Aren't you Annie's boy from Cottondale? What are you doing here in Detroit? Is your family here? Why didn't they let me know they were coming?" The questions rattled out in fury.

It was the reddish-brown complexion of the thin young man that gave away his Indian blood; and the two men were distant cousins.

"Yep, I am Red. Or Rabbit, whatever you want to call me. I came alone, had to leave or those crackers would have killed me."

DB looked him up and down, nodding his head. "You look like you haven't eaten in a week You could use a good meal. Let's go inside and get you something to eat, then we can talk."

Rabbit followed DB into the market. DB asked the butcher slice a pound of bologna, he took a loaf of bread, a jar of mayonnaise from the shelf, and a six pack of grape soda for Rabbit. He took Rabbit to the employee break room.

"Eat first, when you're full, we'll talk."

Rabbit ate all the bologna and half the loaf of bread; he didn't bother to open the mayonnaise. When he was done, he patted his still skinny stomach, wiped his face and looked up at DB. "Thank you so much, DB. You have no idea…."

DB cut him off. "I understand, son. Now, why are you alone in Detroit? How did you get here?"

"I was working on old man Carter's farm. The cracker who was supposed to supervise pushed me for no reason, said I wasn't working fast enough, I turned around and before I could stop myself, I hit him in the mouth and knocked him to the ground. His mouth was bleeding. He yelled, "Nigger, you gone pay for this."

All the colored looked away with panic in their eyes. I left immediately. Told my pa what happened, he gathered a few dollars from friends and family, about $10 in all, Mama made me a lunch with all they were going to have for dinner that night. I put a few things in a sack and said goodbye to Cottondale. Walked at night until I got to Jacksonville, was hanging around the train station when a colored porter saw me and asked me where I was going. Told him I had no money but needed to get up North 'fore they caught me. He got me a ticket and I wound up in Detroit, had heard colored folks could get good jobs up here. So, I got here about a week ago, no money, no place to sleep but safe from those crazy crackers down there. Man, I committed a crime as bad as raping a white woman, I hit a white man."

Placing his hand on Rabbit's shoulder, DB assured him that he was safe now. "Where have you been sleeping?'

"In alleys," said an ashamed Rabbit, his head hanging.

"I have a rooming house for single men where you can stay. And I'll find work for you here at the market for now. They calling you Red or Rabbit?"

"Both. Rabbit cuz the boys said I was as slick and fast as a rabbit and when that Indian blood rose up in me I could protect myself, which I did."

Eventually, DB had Rabbit help him with Miss Josephine's business as well. From that day, Rabbit was DB's man.

Rabbit's Plan

DB's idea excites him, makes him feel like he did when he was enforcer for the Wheel. Keeping track of the competition, or in this case the enemies, gives him a certain thrill. He could be "rabbit" outsmarting those who would make him or those he loves prey, then the "red" would take care of them.

Rabbit's plan was one of surveillance of the three men -- knowing where they were at all times, when and where they took their meals, activities in which they participated, and when they were alone. Rabbit stumbled across a gold mine of information when he catches Maurice smoking a joint behind the shed in the Village Garden. "Taking a break, my man?" snickers Rabbit. An embarrassed and surprised Maurice answers, "Nothing I do often, just today is one of those days, everybody wanting something. You have no idea of what it's like being at the whim and call of someone every minute. Some are nice but many have the devil in them. So, man, if you can, please just forget you saw the brother, would appreciate it."

A smiling Rabbit replies, "No worries, I might even like a hit myself."

With a look of curiosity, Maurice passes the joint to Rabbit. "So, you do still partake," says Maurice as he watches Rabbit take a long pull. "I mean, for a man your age, my elder, I apologize, I am talking too much, a little nervous with you catching me. This place is strict."

"No worries, I fully understand that you have to be steadily on your guard, and you must be pretty good at your job working at this snooty place, if I must say so myself," laughs Rabbit. "What is your position?" inquires Rabbit.

"I was trained as a CNA', replies Maurice."

"Somehow I thought you were a nurse, maybe it's the uniform."

"That is my dream, to get my RN, but it takes more schooling and money of course. This is a good start, especially if I get a good recommendation," volunteers Maurice.

Rabbit's brain starts clicking, strategies from the old days in the numbers racket surfacing like they were used yesterday -- winning folks over to his team. "How much for you to get your RN?" he asks.

"Will take a bit, have to still live while taking classes. I could go to the Technical School or State College here and get it in a couple of years if I didn't have to work." He takes a small toke and passes it to Rabbit. "But I have responsibilities -- separated, with two boys."

Rabbit looks at him for a long minute. Maurice is getting nervous when Rabbit finally speaks. "I just may be able to help you with your dream. Will your dream take about twenty-five thousand?" asks Rabbit.

A shocked Maurice takes a minute to reply. "Man, don't play with me. With that I could get my RN."

"Well, you know nothing is completely free," says Rabbit in a very serious tone, looking directly into Maurice's suspicious eyes. "I can help you if you can possibly help me."

"What do you need? Man, I can't do anything illegal, nothing to mess up my dream of being an RN. No, I can't sell you pot or anything like that."

"What I need from you is information?"

"About?" asks a now curious Maurice.

"Before I get into all of this, Maurice, I see it on your badge. Can I trust you? You can trust me."

After a second of hesitation, Maurice asks, "What information do you need?"

"Three of the residents here…. I will be quite frank with you, it is my understanding that they may have been part of the KKK in Detroit in the old days, the 1930s, when they were young. They may have hurt a good friend of mine. I have their names and need to know absolutely everything about them, from their apartment numbers, to their daily schedule. I simply want to have a talk with them, nothing more. You will not be involved at all," assures Rabbit.

"Wow," say an excited Maurice. "It may take a little time, but I know everyone that works here and have some good friends in high places. What are their names?"

"Earl Lee, Roy Lee and Ray Moses Lee." He sees no recognition in Maurice's face. "I was lucky when I was your age," says Rabbit. "Always worked as an independent contractor, so to speak, for a black group in Detroit, made our own rules. You and I will stay in touch, even enjoy a joint now and then with this old man." The two high five and give each other a brotherly hug. As they move apart, Rabbit holds Maurice's arm. "You talk to no one about this." He walks away.

A Bit More Needed…

In a couple of weeks, Maurice lets Rabbit know that he has the information requested. As a pre-payment, five thousand dollars has been deposited in Maurice's credit union account. With the new information, twenty thousand dollars is placed in his account, a scholarship. from the William Baker Foundation.

Maurice is delighted with the arrangement but a little surprised and alarmed by a second request. "Maurice, my friend needs to be able search the apartments to find information that can be used against the men."

Maurice retorted, "After all this time, you can't try them, no court would take the trial."

"I know, but my friend wants to be absolutely sure so he can let them know he has proof of their involvement."

So, what are you asking me for now?"

Slowly and deliberately, Rabbit replies. "Need three things: one, a skeleton key to be able to enter the apartments; two, information about the security system; and three, any health-related information you may have on the men."

Maurice holds his head down and takes a deep breath. "Man, I don't know."

Rabbit reassures him, "Man, you know I ain't no burglar. I can well afford to live here; it is just crucial to get that information."

Maurice shoots his hand out to shake in agreement to get what Rabbit requests.

"Here is five thousand as a down payment; like before, my friend's Foundation will deposit twenty-thousand dollars in your account as more scholarship money. Maurice, I suggest that you start applying for programs now, so that when you deliver the second request, you can leave this job and go to school fulltime. Of course, both Mr. Bakers and I will provide you with excellent recommendations."

Maurice and Rabbit shake on the deal.

DB is beside himself when he gets the news. He knows that he can always depend on Rabbit. He had done so many years ago in the numbers racket, and now to get the most important thing in his life done, getting justice for his brother Billy.

Maurice gives his two-week notice and goes about his asking. He and Rabbit agree to meet at the mall when the residents are taken there for an outing. Maurice gives Rabbit the security information and the skeleton key. The only one of the three that has a medical issue is Earl Lee. Without being asked, Maurice supplies Rabbit with a hypodermic needle and insulin. A look of understanding passes between the men. Through research, Rabbit learns how much excess insulin will be necessary to cause death.

Choking on the Truth

It is 3 a.m. Everything must be accomplished within a half-hour -- entrance, interrogation, demise. Three soft taps on the door alert DB that it is time for the first kill. Wearing a black and red checkered robe, red pajamas, and tennis shoes, Rabbit stands at the door with a broad smile on his face. Rabbit has always had the propensity for violence. Only because of DB's requirement that the numbers racket be run like a business and not a gang of criminals has Rabbit's violent nature been contained. Now, however, is the time for revenge, and Rabbit is eager to aid DB in the way he can. Besides, Rabbit loves DB like a brother and will do anything to please him. After DB gets out of the rackets, Rabbit squanders his sizable fortune on women, booze, and gambling. When word gets back to DB about Rabbit's financial situation, he gives him a new start under his guidance as he was ever loyal to family, friends, and staff in the racket. Every single person who works for DB during the racket days is given enough money to start a legitimate business, and DB emphasizes saving, as the day might come when the rackets would end. DB pays for the three previous retirement homes in which he, Edward, and Rabbit have resided, and now at Palm Haven. Rabbit not only has his own one-bedroom apartment and gets a monthly allowance.

DB opens the door, a serious look on his face, Edward on his walker follows. The hall lights are turned off at 2a.m., so the trio move slowly down the dark hallway guided only by a flashlight. The men walk quietly and as fast as they can, considering Edward is on his walker and each is over 90 years. They carefully go down two flights of stairs to the third floor on which lives Ray Moses. They walk past doors and entrances decorated with American flags, plants, dolls, and bric-a-brac. Finally, they reach #351, the door plate says *Ray Moses Lee.*

DB eases the key into the socket. Each pulls up his mask. Rabbit enters smoothly and goes immediately to the bedroom; Edward enters slowly but quietly and begins his task in the kitchen. Silence and surprise are their weapons. Rabbit knows the layout of the apartment and stands so as to bar access to the emergency cord. DB quietly disconnects the phone. He shines the flashlight into the sleeping man's face, his mouth slightly agape as a snore escapes. Rabbit now shakes the sleeping Ray Moses roughly and points the 45 in his face. The old man's eyes widen and his mouth opens but no sounds emerge. Terror is all over him.

"Get up, sleepy head," whispers DB sarcastically. Rabbit chuckles.

"What? What do you want?" the old man says as the light blinds him. "How did you get in my apartment?" DB senses the old man's next move.

"Don't do anything stupid like scream if you want to stay alive. I only need you to answer some questions for me."

"Who are you? Questions about what?" Ray Moses is no longer so afraid, and DB can see him plotting.

"Just get up and follow me. Don't forget your glasses," says DB kindly.

Ray Moses slowly emerges from the bed and starts toward the emergency cord. He is stopped by Rabbit. "No tricks, old man. Go into the kitchen right now," demands Rabbit, smiling.

Ray Moses follows the flashlight into the kitchen, eases into the chair pointed to, and then Rabbit pushes him so close to the table that the old man can't move.

"I beg of you, what do you want? I am an old man. If you have come to rob me, I will give you what I have," pleads Ray Moses, looking at each of the men in turn.

"No, I only want answers," says DB. He places a photo of Billy taken the night of his party in 1935. Ray Moses looks at the smiling, handsome Billy and turns away.

"Ever seen him before, Ray?" asks DB mildly.

"No, I never seen him before."

"Are you sure you didn't see him on Christmas Eve, 1935?"

"I am an old man, that's over 80 years ago, how do you expect me to remember a photograph?"

DB places the 1935 police report of finding the body in the field. "Take a good look. You remember when the body was found?"

"Why are you asking me these questions? I know nothing about this," whines Ray Moses.

His attempt to scream is smothered by Rabbit's large, gloved hand. When it's removed, Moses splutters. "Y-you can't blame that on me, we were never tried for that. Someone was lying on us. I am innocent." The old guy weeps. "I-I am an old m-m-man."

"We will be out of your life and let you get back to sleep as soon as you get honest." Rabbit chuckles.

"Please don't' kill me, I am an old man who came here to live out his last years in peace. I was only a kid back then. I didn't mean to hurt anybody. I grew up with colored in West Virginia. I didn't hate no colored. A colored man, Jim, hired my daddy to work for him and even gave us food when we were hungry. I played with them, ate at each other's houses. I never had anything against colored. But in Detroit, things was different, was a lot of hate talk. I listened to it but I knew good colored folks. Please. Forgive me for hurting that colored boy.”

“That colored boy was my brother. He was only 18 years old. He did not deserve to die.”

“I am so sorry.” Ray Moses is now outright crying, wiping his nose on his pajama arm, worried about DB’s reasonable voice.

“Just tell me why you killed him,” DB says, so sadly Rabbit looks at him.

“You don’t understand, it was kill him or get killed myself. I had no choice. You had no choice in the Legion, you did what you were told to do or else you would find yourself dead. Earl said, ‘Do it’, and Roy and I had no choice.” He took a paper napkin out a holder and wiped his eyes. “It weren’t me and Roy, it were Earl, he hated colored.” Ray Moses is weeping uncontrollably again.

“Okay, I understand that,” DB continues to speak reasonably. Moses looks up, his nose running, a weak glimmer of hope in his eyes until DB continues in a different voice. “But why did you leave him half-naked in the snow?”

Ray Moses lowers his head, hope leaking out of him, and says in a whisper, “It was jealously. He was wearing clothes that only rich white men wear. Earl said those clothes was too good for a nig…colored boy. So, he said to take them. I ain't never had no clothes like that, so I took the vest and jacket, then decided to take the shirt, tie and pants as well. Roy like the boots so he took them. And his socks."

"So, what happened to the pocket watch and ring?"

"Earl took the pocket watch and yanked the ring off his finger. Ring had stones in it. "

The trio as if on cue settle their masks down around their shirt collars. Ray Moses gasps. "I got a f-funny f-feeling about you," he stutters out, staring at DB. "the day you had the heart attack, I think you saw the ring. So, what n-now? Are you g-gonna kill me?"

"No, Ray, I am not going to kill you, you are going to do it yourself to make amends for my brother's death."

Edward pushes a plate containing a piece of steak in front of Ray Moses.

No thank you, I don't eat late at night, gives me heartburn."

"It's rib-eye; Just for you," says DB. Rabbit has scanned each month's menus looking for the perfect meal to choke Ray Moses Lee to death.

Rabbit grabs the old man's face and forces his mouth open. Edward shoves the steak into Ray's mouth. Rabbit holds Roy's mouth shut and forces him to swallow. Roy's eyes bulge as he tries to remove Rabbit's hands, He whimpers and finally closes his eyes. DB checks his pulse. Ray Moses Russell is dead so quickly, Rabbit's surprised. And disappointed..

The trio of old men tidy up, leave the plate on the table. They replace the phone on the nightstand, move the chair away from the table a bit, and quietly leave the apartment. They slowly climb the two flights back to the 5th floor. As they exit the stairs, they make sure no aids are around going to a first shift. They quietly enter their apartments. DB pours himself a glass of bourbon and sits on the lanai. He takes a deep breath and exhales. He has hope that he will avenge the murder of his beloved brother before he dies. God has given him another chance. He watches the sun come up. It will be a good day, one of the best in 80 years.

Wash Away the Sins

Even if the killing of the murderers of Billy is too painful for DB, Rabbit knows that justice has is to be done to eventually give DB a sense of peace. He alone, even without Edward, will take care of Roy Lee. As he has done before, Rabbit stakes out Roy, who shows up at breakfast, the gym and the swimming pool at the same time every damned day.

The night he's chosen to act, Rabbit casually walks the corridor, seeing no one at the time of night. Having checked for cameras, he walks up to Roy's door and quietly opens it with a skeleton key. Roy sits on his bed watching television. Something makes him look to his right, and his eyes stretch wide when it registers that it's Rabbit slouched there against the jam. Roy stealthily reaches for the phone, but a pistol pointed at his head changes his mind.

"What do you want nig…?" He catches himself. "If you want money, I have some in the top drawer of the dresser. about a hundred dollars. Get it and go."

"Quiet down. I want you to remain calm and just answer some questions for me. Let's go into the bathroom," says Rabbit.

A confused Roy gets up and shuffles toward the bathroom, turning his head as he goes to keep his eye on Rabbit.

"Now, run a bath, fill the tub." Roy slowly starts to follow orders when he suddenly turns to Rabbit. "I know you." His voice comes out in a squeak. You are one of the three colored guys who're always together. How did you get in here? What is going on? "His voice gets higher and higher.

"Calm down, and I do not want to shoot you. Move away from the alarm, you will be dead before you can push it.," warns Rabbit.

"But, please just tell me what this is about," begs Roy.

"Just fill the tub, get in and soap up good."

"What?" says a now even more concerned and fearful Roy.

"You are going to wash away your sins and ask your Jesus for forgiveness."

"What sins?"

"How many-colored folks did you murder when you were part of the Black Legion?"

Roy's face turns a deep red as his eyes open wide with horror.

"I didn't murder anybody. I work with colored many years, and some of my best friends was colored. Look at me; I'm an old man. I'm like you. What are you talking about?"

"I realize you were a very young man some seventy years ago. But I need you to recall the events of Christmas Eve, December, 1935, when a young colored man was tortured, shot and left naked in a snow-covered ditch in Detroit."

"You got me all wrong, I ain't never killed no colored. Don't remember nothin' like that, no sir."

"Think harder. A young colored man is driving a brand new 1935 forest green coup, he is well-dressed, intelligent and has more than you at the time could have ever dreamed of having."

Roy holds his head down. "Please don't shoot me, I am sorry. Was he related to you? I don't hate colored. Never did. I get caught up that night. It's all my Uncle Earl's idea. We see the car. Beautiful, want to get a closer look. Then we see the colored boy driving, Earl sure he stolen the car from a white. We force him to stop and get out. He get uppity right away, says he's minding his own business and to leave him alone. Earl asks who the car belong to. The guy in the car get smart and say, sassy-like, 'Oh, you think this car is too good to belong to me? Well, it's mine, a gift for graduating from college."

"Lie, lie," Roy whispers. "It's Earl who yells 'Get your nigger ass out of the car.' He won't get out. Earl pull a gun and crash the window. Then we yank the kid out. Earl says, 'We takin' the nigger somewhere to teach him a lesson, to understand how to talk to a white man.'"

"Do you know what you did?" whispered Rabbit. "You destroyed a family, a good man's peace of mind. You threw away the life of a very special boy. I want to hear you ask Jesus to forgive you your sins, lather up and try to wash them away."

A frightened Roy begins to scrub himself furiously. Rabbit scowls and his stone-cold eyes watch the terrified man, which makes Roy start to babble. "I admit Rocky and I beat him as Earl requested but neither I nor Ray Moses shoot him."

"Who pulls the trigger?' asks Rabbit with a kindly smile.

Roy is freaked by the kind voice. "Earl sh-shoot him in the head, tell us to take everything, 'cept the ring, we want from the body. I admit I t-take his boots and socks; Ray Moses gets his clothes, and then we throw him in the ditch.

Rabbit reaches over and with all his strength holds Roy's head down into the full tub of water. Roy struggles but cannot even splash water, let alone match Rabbit's strength. Roy gurgles, and his head remains under water. Rabbit takes a leak, flushes the toilet and sits on the toilet seat for a while to be sure that Roy's dead. He pulls up his trousers, locks the door and returns to his apartment.

The next morning, news of Roy's accidental drowning spreads throughout the village. Earl is nowhere to be seen, and decides that the death of this second nephew is no accident. He makes a call to old friends from the Black Legion and others in Detroit, he gives names of the three black men who live at Palm Haven and requests details about them.

The Confession

Friday's Happy Hour at 3 in the afternoon until 6 is a hit at the Village. Everyone turns out for $1 drinks and free appetizers. Each week a band, DJ, or some other form of entertainment is featured. The trio is sure to make every Happy Hour to keep tabs on Earl Lee now. Earl regularly walks out and sits under the gazebo on the lake after dinner, he is alone now since both his nephews are deceased. DB makes a plan to confront Earl this evening after dinner when he goes to the gazebo. Rabbit insists that he take the hypodermic needled filled with insulin.

The trio greet friends as they enter. The room is packed as usual, but to his utter surprise and delight, Earl Lee is sitting alone on one of the love seats having his drink. DB decides this is the moment, the time to confront him. DB puts on a false smile and does a little colored man's submissive approach to have Earl let him sit next to him. A surprised Earl glares at DB as he sits down. His face reddens, and he shocks DB with the hostility with which the words leave his mouth. "I know who you are, I know all about you and your dealings in Detroit, I know as much about you as you know about me. I too have the means to gather information. I want you to know that I know you are responsible for the murder of my nephews. Their deaths were not accidents. I have written all of this down and placed in a safe place for my family. If anything happens to me, old man, nothing can be done for what happened years ago, but you will spend the rest of your days in prison." DB is taken aback and lets out a deep sigh. His heart is pounding, and for a few moments he is speechless.

But DB's no new rube on the block. He comes to from his slight shock and, in a manner that says they're friends for years, says. "Earl, I don't want to hurt you. We are both old men, and that happened years ago. But before I leave this earth I just need to know why you killed my brother. I only want to finally have peace of mind and hope that at this age, you will be so kind as to give this old colored man relief from his pain. How and why did my brother Billy have to die? What exactly did Billy say or do that made you so angry?"

Earl gets close to DB's face and gloats as he describes Billy's last moments.

Earl clears his throat and smirks. "Your brother did not have to die, he brought it all on himself, the arrogant prick. Better than me, a white man? I keep asking him who the car belongs to and he sticks his black nose in the air and says it's his, a graduation gift from college. I say, 'Yeah, what nigger has a car like this when white men can't even eat these days? Tell me the truth.' He just smiles. I ask him to look at me and tell me who he sees. He looks me straight in the eyes, does not duck his head or nothing and says I am poor ass cracker who hates to see a colored man with more than him. I take the pistol out and point it at his head. Then I tell my nephews to teach him how to respect a white man. Tell 'em to put him on his knees and I give him an opportunity to apologize, I simply ask him to say Mr. Lee, I apologize for my behavior toward you, a white man.' You know what he did? Not look at me, that's for sure; and starts repeating something about 'if we should die, let it be not like hogs…'. I am so angry I shoot him right in that uppity head of his. Now you know what happened and how it could have all been avoided."

DB lets out a deep sigh full of pain and relief.

Sure, my nephews give him a good beating to teach him some manners and yes, I give the permission to take everything from him accept his watch and r…." At that moment, DB's mind begins to race like a locomotive. The ring is the key to getting justice for Billy.

DB, with tears in his eyes, thanks Earl humbly. He even asks if he can get them both another drink, Earl says yes. DB's demeaner surprises Earl, and he himself feels a sense of relief. DB appears to have no anger, just a mild-mannered colored man who understands why his brother has been killed, that it was all Billy's fault that he had to die. DB goes to get the drink. What Earl does not notice is that DB stops to chat with the band director.

After a few tunes and couples dancing on the floor, the band director makes an announcement that one of our residents has something special to tell the group. He points to DB. Earl's heart starts to pound, but he knows he threatened DB with jail if anything happens to him. DB lifts Earl's hand with the ring and starts to talk. Earl's shocked, his heart pounding, and he swallows hard. What can DB possibly want to say?

"Just getting really acquainted with Earl Lee because of this beautiful ring that he is wearing." Earl's eyes widened. "You see, my brother had a ring just like this one. It is from Wilberforce College, a colored school in Ohio. You may have seen this ring on Earl's finger. So, curious, since it was a colored school, I asked Earl how he happened to be wearing this ring like my brother's'. Earl's heart is coming through his chest. "Earl confesses he is a Wilberforce graduate but has been passing for white all these years. He knows that upon graduation as a white man, his life will be different. He requests of me to ask you not to treat him any different. Now that you know he is black, he is the same guy, just pat him on the shoulder and say 'Hi, bro' to him." Let's toast to his confession. Confusion as some raise their glasses and others not. The entire room is now buzzing like a swarm of bees. Earl can barely breathe; he snatches the ring off his finger and throws it on the floor. DB quickly retrieves it and holds it to his heart. Lee's eyes, icy with hate, glare at DB. He stands and bolts from the room, ignoring the chatter, pats on the back, and salutations of 'Hey, brother.' He races to the elevator and collapses at its door. A staff member rushes to him and yells for a call to 911.

The room is filled with chatter.

"All this time -- his whole life! -- he pretends to be white? How about that?"

"Why do you think he finally confessed?"

"I knew there was something about him, he really hated blacks, maybe it was self-hatred."

"I think that is called internalized racism, according to the psychologists."

"His nephews must have been passing too, do you think they committed suicide because they knew he was going to confess?"

"Maybe at this age, he was tired of not being himself."

"There are probably more of them passing than we know."

"Yes, I saw the ring, pretty nice, but never asked about it."

Edward and Rabbit rush to DB. "Man, that was brilliant."

"No need for the hypodermic needle now, give it to me and I will dispose of it" says a giggling Rabbit.

"Did you see his face? I thought the man was going to pass out."

"I thought you were going to let the Village know he was a murderer, but to him, being colored was probably worse."

"Yeah, and white folks would have probably forgiven him for killing a black man but not for fooling them by passing for white."

The trio decided to go to DB's and have their drink rather than stay for dinner. They did not want to answer any questions related to being black. DB told them of the threat that Earl had made but they had no real fears. Word reaches the Village before dinner is served that Earl Lee dies on the way to the hospital.

Probably easier for everyone, a regal white woman says loudly. No awkwardness.

DB tells Edward and Rabbit that it had been a very trying but rewarding evening. He finally knows the truth. He is proud of Billy because he dies a strong black man, he never bowing to Earl. He figures that Billy would have been killed anyway as the envy was overwhelming. DB is finally satisfied that justice has been served for Billy.

But now he has a tightness in his chest and is experiencing shortness of breath. He decides to lie down, but as he looks at the calendar at his bedside, he smiles to himself and writes a note to Billy. DB lays down, and as he looks up from his bed the sees the smiling faces of his father, mother, Granny Ruby, his wife, Miss Josephine, Mother Mary and Billy.

Rabbit and Edward come to DB's apartment to check on him since DB as usual is not in the coffee shop for breakfast. There is no answer, so he lets himself in. DB lies there with a very peaceful look on his face. Rabbit knows that he is gone. He looks down at the note DB writes on the calendar beside his bed; it reads: "Billy, I have gotten justice for you. Numbers are dream makers for Negroes. Tonight, I hit the number, 321, I am one lucky Negro. I have your ring and will give it to you when we meet again." Rabbit looks at the date circled on the calendar, March 21, 321 -- DB's lucky number.

Epilogue

DB's body is taken back to Cottondale, as are all Bakers, and buried in the family cemetery associated with the church his grandfather had helped to found. DB is buried with Billy's ring in his palms. On his tombstone are the words: *A Man Who Possessed A Deep Sense of Love For His People and Who Achieved His Every Goal.*